DeLoMío
Books

THE LAST BODEGA IN JERSEY

Short Stories, Chisme, & More

VOL. I

ABEL VELOZ

"We wish you all the best and pray for the continued success of downtown Jersey City and hope it never forgets its roots and all the small businesses that paved the way."

farewell message from **La Conguita**
1980 - 2015
351 Grove Street, Jersey City

La Conga

352 Grove Street, Jersey City
Permanently Closed on April 16, 2023

Photo: Alexis Agosto
(Jersey City Native)

To the establishments that filled our childhoods, and to legends we shall never forget

RIP - Henry Minyetty & Willy A. Rivas
Champions of their Communities

Part I:
Los Babosos

Stroberi's Intro

STROBERI

La Bodega. The last corner of the block that is still ours. El barrio relegated to seven-hundred square-feet. All of which will be gutted and turned into a gourmet bagel shop after today. We fought hard to keep the store alive, but like grandma says, "The Devil only offers what you can't refuse." Like a quarter-million dollars for a grocery store that has bled red since the Walmart opened.

When I lock up tonight, it will be the last time. The end of an era. No more quarter-juicies, which are now fifty-cents. No more arguments with the customers over the price of plátanos. Now the verdes turn into maduros; and the maduros into fly traps. It's just not the same anymore. But the remaining vecinos still come in for their EBT and WIC needs. And of course, for their loosies, lottery tickets, and deli sandwiches.

I fling the storefront gate upwards. It rattles like a train on tracks until hitting the top. I take one look left and right.

The block is calm. Occupied by the tumble and crinkle of litter and the buzz of the streetlights. Nobody in sight. More importantly, no stick-up boy catching the early worm (me). This really is the last day. I take a deep breath. The last bodega in Jersey City. Wow. Just thinking it sounds wild. Like the start of a dystopian world.

I sigh.

Maaaaaan, what am I talkin' 'bout? Fuck this bodega! Never wanted to be here in the first place. I inherited it from my Pops last year. His dying wish was that I continue serving the community. Well, the community never served me. They've only given me a jail sentence. Because that's what owning a bodega is, a jail sentence. Clock in at 6AM; clock out at 10PM. Listening to the same bachata, salsa, and balada mixtapes over and over. Dealing with the same clowns every day.

You know how many tecatos I've kicked out of this store? Too many. Every day at least one. And if I was unlucky enough, I'd kick out the same one five times in one day. Do you know how hard it is to reason with someone whose eyes are looking one way, lips babeando the other way, while their mind is orbiting the planets? Yo, like I mean, what the fuck!? I rather play La Gallina Ciega with a used diaper as my blindfold.

I'm too young for this. I should be in college. Studying some smart shit. Whispering Romeo Santos lyrics into the ears of educated women. Not these raised by wolves, Cardi B wannabe's that come in here saying, "what up, son?" or, "good looks, my nigga." I cringe every time.

That's why tonight, at 7PM, when the Jew comes with the papers, I'm signing the deal. Sorry, Pops. The community ain't worth more than a quarter mill'.

I flick on the lights. I close my eyes waiting for G-Hombre, the bodega cat. Yep, that's his name. G like the letter G, and Hombre like the Spanish word for man. His real name is Giambi, named after Jason Giambi from the A's and Yankees. But the way my dad would say it, the cat responds to nothing but G-Hombre. "G-Hombre, what you got for me today?" I call out.

It's our morning ritual. I walk in, and he gifts me the trophies from his night's hunt. Tom and Jerry shit. A mouse or two that crawled its way down from the apartments upstairs. Only caveat is I gotta keep my eyes closed until he's done. And from the sound of it, he put in work last night. I hear him bouncing wall to wall, brushing past the chips.

He goes silent. Must be everything. I open my eyes.
WHAT. THE. FUCK.

This the shit I'm talkin' 'bout. Fuck this place! Like, really? I cross my arms. I should have never let those teenagers use the bathroom. Kids can't smash at home, so they think they can smash here. A used condom next to a baby mouse.

"Last day," I mutter to myself.

I stretch on latex gloves, scoop the *trophies* and dump it in the trash outside because one thing about customers, they nosey. Before they even step a toe in here, they appraise the place. Ready to complain about anything and everything that has nothing to do with them.

Second thing about customers, they could all be fiction writers if they turned their exaggerations and mouths into pens. See a mouse in the trash and they'll assume Fievel and his whole American Tail live here. See the used condom and they'll think I'm smashing the whole vecindario. *I heard it was Juanita. Nah, I heard it was Juanita's mom. Nah, it was Juanita's cousin that came from New York last week. The one with the fatty.* The rumor when I took over the bodega was, *He is going to turn it into a hookah lounge.* All because I put on un dembow: music my dad never allowed. But you also have to laugh at the nonsense and admire it at the same time. These customers can turn one fleeting glance from a stranger into a tale about a stalker. Probably the only thing I'll miss about this place. The stories.

The door chimes open.

"Scooby-doo PA-PA! Y el Caco Pelao suena RA!" a man with way too much energy, pushing a baby stroller, says. His baby half-asleep. "Stroberi? Naaaa, that can't be you?" He smiles wholeheartedly.

Damn, he said my birth name (My dad's attempt at naming me after Darryl Strawberry).

"Look at how you've grown. I know it's been a hot minute, but I dreamt about your Pops yesterday so I had to come visit."

At the crack of dawn? I look at him and his baby.

The man catches the judgement in my eyes. "Don't worry about the baby. She's nocturnal. My baby-moms hit the clubs during her pregnancy, so she only falls asleep if she out en la calle." He adjusts the baby's blanket, then looks around in nostalgia…or in judgement, tit for tat. Although today, I wouldn't be offended. It's the last day, and I took the liberty of being extra lazy with restocking.

"Wow, even though it's been a minute, this place doesn't change. Where's the old Caco Pelao? He in the back?"

"Dead."

"Oh. What? When?"

"About a year ago. The doctors said it was kidney failure. I think it was the sixteen-hour-a-day bachata-balada diet he was on. All that amargue."

He rubs the nape of his neck in embarrassment, then chuckles. "I guess that's a way to go out. But my bad. Didn't know." He purses his lips, wrestling with what to say next. "By the way, you probably don't remember me. I'm Yoskar. Your Pops did me a huge favor back in the day. 'Bout ten years ago, when you was what? Ten? Nine?" He lets out a hearty exhale. Pushes the stroller directly across from me at the register.

I can tell my Pops meant something to him. Especially with how chill he's leaning on the ice cream fridge. Like he owns the place. Like he spent many hours talking to my Pops in this same exact position.

"Damn, I missed his funeral." He shakes his head.

"Don't worry, you can still pay your respects. His body

is buried at Bay View, but his spirit remains here. Your pick." It's not a lie. Sometimes I sense my Pops in here. His devotion sprinkled all over the fridges, shelves, and crates like ashes. Especially behind the counter. I call it the viewpoint of his life. "If you don't mind me asking, what my Pops do for you?"

"What do you mean?" He quickly takes out his phone and starts texting away. Once he notices my pause, he says, "My bad. Just needed to send an urgent text."

"You said he did you a favor."

"Pshh," he swipes the air with his phone, "saved my life."

My dad saved this man's life? *Yeah aight.* I can sense exaggeration from a mile away, but that doesn't make me any less intrigued. "Well, as you can see, the bodega is empty and the crackheads haven't resurrected yet," I say, inviting him to tell the story.

He chuckles. "I see you a funny guy, just like your dad."

"Ehh. I'm just more of an asshole." We exchange nods of amusement.

"Where do I start? I was eighteen and thought I could finesse anything. It had always been that way. Always managed to get out of situations. But this situation, let's just say it went downhill once I showed up at my ex's baby shower."

"You showed up to your ex's baby shower?" I laugh.

"Peep it." His hands move in a rhythmic manner: the sign of a good storyteller. "I showed up, right. Pshh. Pa qué fue eso."

Yoskar's
Baby Shower Novela

YOSKAR

It's not that I didn't care. It's that back then, I'd rather observe self-sabotage—including my own.

That's why I decided to show up at my ex's baby shower. Can you believe she was dating my uncle? Couldn't even mention Vida as my ex anymore. It invited the jokes: "Damn kiddd, I guess she found better." Yeah, okay. The only thing she found was a way to cover up our situation.

My girlfriend at the time, Carolina, was also invited. But she wasn't with the shits. Couldn't understand why I'd show up. "Yoskar, you'd have to be a top-class sinvergüenza to attend your ex's baby shower. And what would they say about me, huh?"

But she was tripping. To turn down un chivo al fogón and the opportunity to prove that my ex definitely didn't find better…over pride? Na, na, na. That type of bundle doesn't come often enough. Plus…the baby was mine.

"Ayo, Boobie!" I shouted across our section of the park.

This was Lincoln Park, by the way. Back when even the underaged could get away with sippin' responsibly.

And Boobie is Vida's younger brother and my best friend till this day. Turned out to be an aight uncle. Which I doubted at first 'cause he had this whole Robin Hood thing going on. He stole from people that showed off on Facebook. You flash it—I find you—then I snatch it, his motto. Earlier that week, he five-fingered a baby pair of Guccis for me—my baby shower gift. (Oh, and clearly, the baby you see in this stroller right now isn't the same baby. I see the quick expression of confusion dissipate off Stroberi's face.)

Now, whose baby got robbed? Don't ask me irrelevant questions. You know how it be. In this neighborhood, you only ask if someone will come looking for it. Which in Boobie's case, never happened. He stole from the rich side of the city, near Exchange Place. And by the sight of the Starbucks across the street, this might be becoming a rich side too, but that's not the point.

"Yerrr." I attempted to get Boobie's attention. But between the dembow boinging off the subwoofers and the bochinche climaxing at every table, it was a difficult task. So what I do? I clacked two beer bottles. One that I chugged at arrival. The other, I babysat till it matched that day's scorching temperature, half full. The clacks got the whole party's attention. I swear the trees shifted their branches my way too.

"Ew. What's he doing here?" someone who sucks at whispering, said.

Why was I there? Okay, reasonable. But ew? Maaan, I didn't reply to that. It was probably one of Vida's crusty-ass friends. And I wasn't gonna let them get a reaction out of me. So I avoided all the what-the-fuck-is-he-doing-here stares and focused on Boobie's peanut head. "While you over there, get me another beer," I shouted.

Boobie tossed his hands up, gesturing he had no clue what I said.

I couldn't blame him 'cause the baby shower was jumping like a Dominican Independence Day festival. Which forced a game of charades between us.

I pointed at the makeshift cooler: a trash-can lined with a plastic bag.

He stepped closer to it, then looked at me for confirmation.

I made a fist, pinky and thumb out, and mimicked a chugging motion.

He pointed at a nearby baby bottle.

You get the point. This guy is a fucking idiot. If anyone needed some milk, it was him. Dude was slenderer than a Black & Mild.

I jabbed my index finger at the garbage can again.

He busted out in laughter. The constant joking around, another uncle trait he checked off.

And no, no, no, no, no, NO. I would never let another man raise my child, if that's what you were thinking. My father always said he won the lottery when I got a stepdad. As if God blessed his irresponsibility. But like I said, I rather observe self-sabotage. With the extra free time, he was getting milked dry by a girl roughly my age. (She was legally of age, though. I had seen her driver's license and fake ID.) But that situation is not important either.

Whereas my father pawned me off to my stepdad for a playboy lifestyle, I only planned on taking sabbatical. You know. Spend a few years away to experience life and attend Princeton the following year. The early admission letter arrived a week prior. And the way I saw it, Vida's boyfriend, aka my Uncle Perc', could play daddy till then. 'Cause dude persevered past addiction, so he could definitely persevere through a Maury "You are NOT the father" experience.

So as you can see, this whole situation was fucked up. Was it my fault? I'll let you decide.

Then Boobie handed me a beer and dragged a chair next to me.

"Good looking out," I said. I leveraged the bottle cap off with my wedding band.

(Oh yeah, I was married too. Wasn't hiding that. Just didn't want you to think I was that type of guy. Which I'm not. A friend of a friend of a friend needed papers, and I always plan ahead. Married for that Princeton money. Carolina was cool with that. Vida wasn't. And the only reason I kept the wedding band on was in case Immigration Services pulled up on me.)

Boobie placed a heavy hand on my shoulder. He had this energy to him. 'Cause honestly, I expected him to be on his third round of "no me importa que usted sea mayor que yo, age is just a number" in one of Vida's friend's ears. That's how I knew something was off.

"Do you ever wonder," he focused on Vida sitting on her white, woven throne, surrounded by baby blue balloons, "that that could be you next to my sis, instead of Perc'? Baby and everything?"

Yes. No. Maybe. Shit, he knows!? I thought.

"Come on, bro." I nudged him like he said something outlandish. "You over here wishing me to be a baby daddy at eighteen. Let me get through senior year first. Shit, let me get through this *beer* first." I gulped past the bottleneck. I chuckled; he didn't.

"I'm just saying. I did the math—"

I cupped his mouth shut. For a sec, I thought he inherited Walter Mercado's powers because that's one secret I never told. And I know Vida wouldn't. They were the type of siblings that avoid each other at all costs. Which was impressive on their part. Whenever I'd visit Vida, we'd be locked up in her room (how she got pregnant). Then when I'd go to Boobie's room next door, it would be like I was in a different house. But all I knew was, I couldn't have any of those chismosos hearing his words. If that happened, the entire Greenville section of Jersey City would know, like they all tuned into the same emisora.

"Chill out, Boobie. Remember how you failed Algebra?"

He nodded until he caught onto what I was insinuating. That his math was off. And that Vida was seven months pregnant. And we only broke up seven months prior. The day I got married.

"Fine. You got me." I released his mouth. "You know my other situation." I leaned in closer. "If it's mine, I won't abandon him. Believe that. But again, you know my situation. And I rather be an absent father than a dead father."

And that was reality. I got myself into an entanglement. Ensnared myself into a novela-type situation. If I declared my son, there was no telling what my wife and Carolina would do. Have me tossed into the Hudson River? Snip off my you-know-what and let me bleed out? If I stayed hush, I'd get to live as a deadbeat father. And as you can see, I'm still alive.

"Yeah…" Boobie heavy-sighed, then looked at Vida again. And that's the one thing everyone understands: death. Doing the right thing, after doing a wrong thing, can get you killed sometimes. He knew that, I knew that, and I'm sure you know that.

So I followed suit by looking Vida's way, keeping my eyes one foot behind her toward the bandejas. That way nobody could report anything to Carolina. Especially since I received a text notification from her just moments prior. If anyone reported anything, I'd say, Chill, I was looking at the food.

I watched Vida go table to table. People rubbing her belly, feeling the kicks. Which fun fact, those were not kicks at all. He was adjusting his feet in the batter's box. Like father, like son. The thought sneaked a smile out of me, but it was quickly snatched by my uncle trailing behind her. He stared me dead in the eye and gestured an I-see-you with his fingers. Then BAM! I got snuffed off my chair. I was on the dirt thinking, how the fuck he know telekinesis? But when I looked up, it was the devil herself, my girlfriend.

I had an all-white outfit until Carolina had me looking like I stole second, third, and home base.

"We ignoring texts now, huh?" Carolina barked.

"Chilllll, I was looking at the food." Why the fuck I say that? Knowing damn well that the aluminum was still on everything and the fogón was not in a finessable distance. Knowing damn well I didn't even answer her question.

I didn't tell you, but Carolina could box. On this very corner outside of the bodega, she laid some crisp combos on a few girls. Like too crisp. Did the whole breathing thing too: tss-tss tss-tss-tss.

I panicked. I grabbed my beer off the floor. Chugged it and said, "*Relax*." Said it like I was in control too. But we know what that word does to Latinas. So why I say that?

Like I said, it's not that I didn't care. It's that I'd rather observe self-sabotage—including my own.

Tss-tss tss-tss-tss...

STROBERI

I was waiting for Yoskar to continue, but he just stopped and started checking on his baby.

"Wait-wait-wait. That's it? The end?"

"Yeah, man. She knocked me out."

"Sheesh." That's wild. But that's the least of my intrigue. "What happened to your son? Your ex? Exes? Uncle? And how did my dad save your life?"

Yoskar leans harder against the ice cream fridge and exhales. "Bro, it was never my son. My ex cheated on me with my uncle in hopes that the baby would look like me at birth, forcing me to stay. And you see, my uncle was younger than my father. And I already told you about my father's playboy lifestyle. So my uncle followed his example. He told me, 'Sobrino, I did you the favor. Saved you from one that belonged to the streets. You owe me.' He was all about those words till Vida turned out pregnant. He even offered me the tuition money if I would take his place. But I wasn't falling for that. Never trust a desperate man's promise. When I chose to marry for the tuition money, he took the L and did the responsible thing. Covered that whole scandal up."

"So who's your baby moms?"

Yoskar chuckles. "You really want to know?"

Of course. Who doesn't mind a good chisme? I nod.

"My uncle's side piece." He shimmies his shoulders before dusting himself off. "My uncle is like my father, so I knew he'd get a new youngin' eventually. Waited nine long years for my opportunity." He extends a fist-bump my way with the grin of a champion.

Okaaay? I hesitantly dap him up. That explains the nocturnal-baby thing. The moms is still just trying to experience life.

"So what exactly did my dad do for you?"

"Like I said, he saved my life. I was at the baby shower, concussed. Boobie was scared to call 9-1-1 because he procured half of the baby shower gifts. And that's one thing rich people and gentrifiers don't hesitate on: calling the cops. That stuff was likely reported stolen. Add on the fact that my uncle was semi-estranged from my fam because of his past drug habits. So there was nobody on my side. When I tell you I saw about twenty phones out, it was probably more like fifty. Everyone recording, nobody calling.

"Luckily, your Pops closed the store for thirty minutes 'cause he heard on the block that there was a chivo al fogón at the park. Even more enticing was that somebody's aunt flew in the caldero from DR. So he knew there wouldn't be none of the metallic residue from the cheap American ones. Your dad didn't even call 9-1-1. He filled up his cantina and drove me to the hospital." He tilts his head to show me a scar on the back of it. "I was leaking."

"El Diablo!" I blurt out. "She tried to give you that Harry Potter design too."

"Yep. But listen," he looks around the bodega, "after that Monchy y Alexandra/Pimpinela episode, me and your Pops became tight. I'd show up with a few brews here and there and we'd just shoot the shit. Listen to music, tell stories.

And your dad had a ton of those. Dude never ran out of them. I'm sure he told you enough stories to write a bible's worth. Old and New Testament."

Truth be told, he didn't. He spent so much time in this place that by the time he got home, he would just shower and sleep.

"That man had stories for days," I lie. Well, it's not a lie because he probably did. He just never told me many. Only barked orders. "Stroberi, you need to work harder at school. Stroberi, you need to focus on the important things. Stroberi, I didn't come to this country for you to be on the computer all day." Stroberi, Stroberi, Stroberi, never followed by any words of positive encouragement.

"I tell you, without stories like the one I just told you, what's life?"

What's life? Life is not getting cheated on with your uncle. I chuckle inside my head. But I understand where he's coming from. You can only have stories if you live. And that dampens my mood. "I'm too young to know about life. I just know it's not in this bodega." I sigh. "In here, you live vicariously through others. I haven't taken a weekend off since I took over this place. Can't even afford an employee, let alone pay myself a respectable wage."

Yoskar doesn't say it, but his face turns into a silent, "Oh…" Taking pity on me. "Hey," he rummages for consoling words but as soon as he can't find one he checks his phone, eyes blaring open after reading a notification, "don't mean to be abrupt, but I gotta go. Like now. And as you can see, the sun is basically out, and la nena needs a real bed now. Which means I can finally knock out too." He hits me with an unnecessary double shot of I-gots-to-go. But before he does, he pensively looks at the ice cream fridge and taps it. "I should have come around more often, but Vida still lives on the block and ain't nobody got time for that."

"In any case, thanks for stopping by. The man above is surely smiling. Bald head shining and everything," I say, in an attempt to lighten the mood.

We shake each other's hand. And as he pushes the stroller out of the bodega, he says, "And good luck. You gonna need it."

"What?" I heard him but that last part was awkward: You gonna need it. Sounded more like a threat.

I won't say Yoskar's nostalgic looks around the bodega made me do it, but I couldn't let the bodega go out like that. Looking all barren. So I got to it: locked and loaded the coffee machine, restocked the sodas and waters. Set everything up just like my dad would. With pride. With respect. But this time, it felt ritualistic. I didn't just throw everything in its place, I was intentful.

I flick on the OPEN neon lights and mosey behind the counter. And if I'mma be intentful, I gotta do what my Pops would do on a typical day. I unzip the burned CD binder full of all the music that as a child I hated, but as an adult I'm starting to appreciate. I could just plug in my phone—is what I wanna tell myself as I scrounge through the binder—but that wouldn't be fitting for the last day. Today, we shall start wiitttthhh…fuck it. A little Monchy y Alexandra is a fitting interlude between Yoskar's visit.

As I press play on the store's relic of a stereo, the door smacks open, the chimes somersault on its hook. A woman with a tubi, in her bra, leggings, and furry slippers huffs and puffs. She franticly steps in and out of the store's three aisles. "Where is he!?"

Here we go with the crackheads. Although she doesn't quite have the look. I'm also sure I've seen her around with her son. Junior is his name, I think. "Calm down, Captain Chonga. Where's who?" I quickly lower the music, and sneakily reach for the baseball bat next to the stereo.

Her face crinkles like a Pitbull ready to pounce. "Captain Chonga? Oh you funny, huh? Where the heck is Yoskar? I got a text saying he was here. Where is he?" She points at the bathroom door. "Is he in there?" She swings open the door. "Come out, B—"

"Ayo. Cójelo con take it easy." I now have a firm grip on the bat.

How in the world did someone know Yoskar was here? It was only me, him, and G-Hombre. I look outside the storefront glass, while keeping my peripherals on the crazy lady. There isn't a soul in sight. So who—

The image of Yoskar texting mid-convo rushes to mind.

I chuckle, but quickly catch myself. My amusement would be snitching. But not like it matters.

Outside a car double parks. The front-passenger window zips down. "BUT TODAY I GOT TIME! HA. GOT EEEEEM!" Yoskar peels off.

My chuckle reemerges into full-blown laughter. This lady must be Vida. And now I'm really confused. For this lady to be here this early and this mad, Yoskar must have fed me some bullshit. But this shit hilarious.

And that's another thing I'll miss about this bodega. Why hop on Worldstar or The Shade Room when you can just watch the block? The pettiness, the comedy, the novela that films itself 24/7 like there is a hex deep in the bodega's foundation, inviting the local drama. It's just always better when the drama doesn't involve you.

"And what the fuck are you laughing at?" Vida says, as she scuttles out of the store, then launches after the car for a few desperate strides, leaving one slipper behind. "YOS-KARRR!!!! I'M GOING TO KILL YOU!"

Yikes. She sounded like she meant that, too.

Ahhh, shit. She's coming back.

"Let me tell you something," she says in an authoritative tone.

Anda el diablo. Here it comes.

The Bodega Kardashians

STROBERI

The morning rush came in and out. All fifteen customers buying anything with bread, accompanied by a cheap cup of coffee or energy drink. It doesn't help that there's a new Starbucks on the other corner, but when that line is bussin', we get a few gringo stragglers. Fortunately, Vida had run her mouth dry before they came in. And by they, I'm talking 'bout the local news station.

"Wait. So let me get this straight. Your actual name is Strawberry?" the news reporter, a middle-aged woman with a lift job or two, says.

"No, it's Stroberi. Stro like the Astros. Beri like a toddler saying, berry, very delicately."

"Stra—"

"Just call me Pelao Jr." I cut her off before she struggles with it again. It's what people on the block have called me since forever due to my strong resemblance to my father, or because it's a convenient way of addressing me without having to recall my actual name.

"Pe-Pe-Loud Jr.," the reporter says. "I got it right, right!?"

No, bitch. "Yep, that's it." I fake-smile. "Just lose the d at the end of loud."

"And Giambi is the cat's name?" She points at G-Hombre laying on the top shelf of the canned goods section.

"Why do you need him again?"

"For the ratings. People love when cats do anything."

"Good luck with that. He about to do a whole lot of nothing."

"We're rolling in five, four, three…" the cameraman counts down.

I clear my throat and flatten out my eyebrows, anticipating the camera. Only now realizing that I have no clue why they're here. "Wait, why—"

"Good morning, Hudson County. This morning, we are live at Cibao Deli & Grocery, thee, I repeat, thee last bodega in Jersey City. I'm here with Pelao Jr, the young owner of the bodega, and his very well-fed bodega cat, Giambi, the ex-Yankee." She forces a chuckle. "Pelao Jr, tell us about the history of this bodega. And why, out of all the bodegas, this is the last one?"

Sheesh! Wish I could've prepped for this. The simple answer is that my dad was too stubborn to sell a failing business. He found honor in sinking with the ship. But I can't say that. I'll just wing it. I'll let my Dominican demonio—natural slick talk—do the talking. I'm not even nervous.

"The bodega—by the way, don't get it twisted with a grocery store or a deli, we are more than that—was my father's, who was known as Caco Pelao because of his pristine bald head. I mean, you could rub it once and three genies would poof out of there. You know what I'm saying?" This bitch don't have a clue what I'm saying. She just smiling, looking at me enthusiastically.

"He immigrated here in the 90s with the dream that he'd make a living here."

"The American Dream, I see," the reporter says. She glances at the camera, then back at me.

"The American Dream? Na, the American Nightmare. We all know the deal. No need to fluff it for the audience," I say. "Anyway, my Pops—"

"YERRRRRR. What it do babbbyyyyy?" my cousin, Rico, parades into the bodega, unaware of the camera. I cringe. He daps me up, then overtly checks out the news reporter. "Oh, we on TV?" He tucks on the exposed ends of his durag, then fixes his Yankee fitted.

"As you can see, a loyal customer has joined us. What's your name, young man?"

"I'm Rico." He hangs an arm around my shoulder and sways me side to side in a hip-hop bop. "Ayo, rest in peace Lil' Lisa, Young Buddha, Ceecee. Shout out to my peoples in the Heights. JC Heights, not the Bronx. YERRRRR, we out here. I made it, Ma. Your son a star." Rico performs a spin move, then announces that he is going to make himself a sandwich.

The reporter forces another chuckle. "You heard Rico. Shout out to his peoples, who are joining us at home."

"Na, yo. They don't watch the news," he half-attentively says, behind the deli counter, "they lurk on TikTok and Twitter."

That's actually very factual. Ever since the side-scrolling school closure information moved online, there hasn't been a need to watch live news. All they ever show are the bad things that happen in the hood or white people *doing* good things in the hood. So why watch it? We've got front-row seats to that. "Anywho, as I was saying before my cousin interrupted—"

"Wait, just so it's clear. This is a family business? Your cousin, Rico, works here too?" The camera pans out towards Rico stroking turkey through the slicing machine.

"Him? Naaaaa. He is what we call a lambón."

"Ayo, who you calling a lambón?"

"You, you fool."

"What's a lambón?"

"A free-loader. But he blood. And family must always eat. So calling him a lambón is basically my way of coping with the idea that he never brings anything to the table." I can hear Rico smack his lips at my comment.

"Yeaaahh, aiiggghtt," he murmurs.

The reporter laughs. "I've only been here for ten minutes, and I've already learned what a bodega cat is and a lambón." She turns back to the camera. "I'm sure we all know one of those." She chuckles. "Reporting live from *thee* last bodega in Jersey City, I'm Carla Rossi with JCNJ News, and I look forward to seeing everyone back here soon." The camera lowers and without a moment's pause, Carla claps ecstatically.

"Guys, just heard from the studio. Ratings are off the chart! The producers love the dynamic between you two. That whole little bickering moment was prime time. Can we get more of that?"

More of that? "Thought y'all were here to cover the bodega? The important stuff. 'The pillar of the immigrant community,' my father would say. A dying community, as you can see. New condominiums. Zone parking. Rent so high that long-time residents were forced out. Higher property taxes. The Starbucks across the street was the final puzzle piece." And little does Carla know, this is *thee* last bodega's *last* day.

The reporter seems unbothered. "That all sounds interesting, but we found something better. You two! And word from our sponsors is that they are willing to pay for their products to be placed in the background. How does one-thousand dollars sound?"

"One-thousand?" I question if it's for real. I glance at Rico pressing his sandwich in the sandwich press. Would have to slide him a hundo or two. Of course, I'd deduct that sandwich out of his cut. Something isn't right, though. "You want more of me and Rico...bickering? Wouldn't that be like reality TV? Like a Bodega Kardashians." If so, I don't know how I'd feel about that.

"Reality TV and the news…same thing," Carla says smugly. "The audience never knows the difference."

And that's exactly the motha-fuckin' issue. People see all the bad stuff in the hood and believe that's reality. But a stack just to put some product on my shelves? Say less. But to be someone else's entertainment? I don't know about that. Luckily there aren't enough vecinos left to say I sold out the community. This doesn't feel right, yet… "For two-thousand, y'all can put whatever y'all want in the background." There gotta be more money where that came from.

"Deal," she accepts without deliberation.

Shit! Should have asked for more.

"We'll draft up the paperwork. Who knows, we might even make this an hour-long special! *The Last Bodega in Jersey, the End of an American Dream*." She spreads her hands out, visualizing the title. "Yep. It could work. We'll start setting up as soon as we get the equipment."

"Wait, so what exactly is going to happen?"

"It's simple. Conduct business as usual. We'll record for a few hours, and hopefully in those hours we capture a day in a bodega."

Sounds simple enough. If all I gotta do is conduct business as usual, this should be light work.

While Carla Rossi and the cameraman retreat to their news van, I check out what Rico is doing. Gotta make sure he isn't making another two-pound sandwich to go. I also gotta inform his broke ass about the business proposition. But from the look of him, I think he already heard.

"Ayo, Pelao, peep this."

Oh, boy. Here we go. What scheme he coming up with now? Rico always wants to turn a great situation into a once-in-a-lifetime situation. Like last year, when he finally hooked up with his crush since third-grade, but before he reached third base, he tried to turn that into a three-some with her best friend. *Tried* being the key word.

"Do you know anything about generational trauma? It's been on my mind for a couple of days," he says. The last thing I'd expect to come out of his mouth. "Last week, I went to Rutgers New Brunswick with Arismeldy and Jacinto. Ended up in some willlld frat house. But before all that, some shortie-rock gave me hella book recommendations. I bought one of them, and it was legit. It explained generational trauma. You smart, I need your take on it."

"Wait-wait-wait, you read a book? How did that happen?" I ask. "Forget it. You already said it. A girl."

He laughs in embarrassment, turning his fitted cap backwards. "My moms always said I should go to college. So I went to Rutgers for a party and left with an education. A whole ass scholar. Check it—"

"Na-na-na. Check nothing. This better not be one of your long-winded stories with commercial breaks."

"Chill, cuzzo. Just hear me out..."

COLLEGE BOYS FOR THE NIGHT

RICO

How the heck was I supposed to know that she was gender binary, non-binary, or whatever math equation she claimed to be? I was just trying to holla at the chick.

I said, "Ayo mamiiii, let me change your life for a sec." Something light. Not original, but it's not like I said what I really wanted to say. But that's what I get for not being direct.

She went on to ask me a million questions. "What do you mean by change my life? And why only for one second? You don't look rich. Do you even go to this school? And why did you call me mommy?" All questions I wasn't used to—you know how it be. You catcall and the shortie either ignores you or smiles. But not this educated mamasota.

When I attempted to halt her onslaught, she gave me ten book recommendations: something about love languages, self-healing, another about self-respect. I wrote them down in order to seem interested so that she would give me the digits. But after I looked them up, I realized she was either dissing me or educating me. In any case, Jacinto and Arismeldy were not impressed.

"So you telling me, you was jotting down book titles, not the digits?" Jacinto asked. He rocked side to side, flat-footed. Keeping warm and not creasing his Jordans.

"Told you, bitch! No Twitter name, IG, or Snap is that long. Now pay up!" Arismeldy rubbed his thumbs together.

Arismeldy then went on a mini rant about how college girls are a different breed. That we would never bag. "Not even Rico is gonna bag." Those were his exact words. So you already know I took that as a challenge. 'Cause pimpin' runs through our veins, naw mean?

(Woooow, one camera comes in here and you start acting brand new? Better go apologize to your Pop's dick when you visit his grave, 'cause now you frontin' on his name. Whatever. Damn, thinking about it now, I should have told the snow bunny that my name meant rich. I sigh. We live and we learn.)

"Pssh. Yeah, yeah, yeah. I'm just warming up," I said to Arismeldy's hating-ass.

The night was young, so I believed that. It was like 10PM. But the Arismeldy broken record of negativity kept spinning. "Yo, we really trying to meet this frat house's random three-girls-per-guy ratio? This type bullshit."

That's when I assumed he wasn't thinking. If each guy walked in with three girls, imagine how many girls would be puti-suelta inside.

"Negativo. Must be a bunch of dudes inside with no punani in sight. A Vienna sausage can. That's why they got us hustling cheeks for them," Arismeldy said.

He kinda had a point. On the block, if we rounded up nine girls, we'd just throw our own lil' shin dig. And maybe... *maybe* invite two to three more homies as reinforcement.

"I'm talking to you too." Arismeldy nudged Jacinto, who was busy scrolling up and down his phone. "Them looking for more girls means there are too many dudes and…shoot! You already know that's cool with me." Arismeldy began sexy-walking to the music vibrating out of the frat house. You know how he been acting ever since he came out. Most moments he himself until he loses control of his femininity. This bi-polar switch from Debo to Ru Paul.

"Chill, bro. We get it. You're gay," Jacinto said. "Now channel into your gay snake-charm shit and make instant female friends so we can get out of this cold."

Arismeldy said no words, just a very easy to understand look-of-death.

"Whatever, man." Jacinto slapped the air in discontent. "While y'all figure it out, I'mma keep lurking on the dating apps." He sat down on a nearby bench.

So that's when I asked Arismeldy if he had any ideas. So we lent our attention to the frat house that, at second glance, looked like an upscale crack house. It just looked… gross. Giant wood-carved Greek letters on the porch that were desperate for a fresh coat of paint. The hardly maintained lawn. I didn't even have to touch the step's railings to know that it could break like a WWE prop. Several dangling wood panels on the roof. I could hear the floorboards creaking from outside. House just looked worn down. And something about its faded, chipped paint exterior gave it damp, sticky vibes. But that was the spot I needed to get into.

"We could pretend to be bros," Arismeldy suggested.

Another broken record. I've told him too many times before that we brothers for life and that blood wouldn't make us any tighter. Not even rubbing our dicks to start a fire would. But apparently he wasn't seeking affirmation—something else I read about.

"Whoa," he slowly said, shocked and amused at the same time.

Aight, I admit. I OD'ed with the dicks comment but still.

"I was talking 'bout pretending to be frat bros. You know, the token-minority recruits from the semester Black Lives Matter mattered. I haven't seen a single shade of brown or black come in or out of there. Why we even trying to get into this party? You into EDM now?"

"Ayooooo." Jacinto stood on the bench, ran in place, jumped off the bench, then ran circles around us, shouting a bunch of *Yooo*'s and *Dammmmmn*'s. "Just swiped YES on guess who?" He dribbled his eyebrows.

"Your moms," Arismeldy joked.

"It's way better than that." He started two-stepping and waving his hands in the air, side to side. Then he started singing the intro to Usher's "My Boo," dragging out the anticipation.

"Just say it, you mojón" I said.

"Bethany!" Jacinto launched into another round of laps.

"Beth-who?" I pretended to not make the connection. But I knew exactly who he was talking about.

Remember the shortie I was in love with? The one I almost smashed, but told me I needed to put in more effort? Correction, *any* type of effort. I hadn't given up on that. So driving an hour to see her was me putting in the effort. Wanted to surprise her. Show her that I was a man that knew what he wanted. And I wanted all of her. The whole cuatro golpes. The combi completa. Like bro, she is mad chill, watched all of Dragon Ball Z, and got the juiciest culazo I've ever seen on a white girl.

(Aight, Stroberi. Don't fall asleep on me yet. I promise on Tío's bald head that this story is going somewhere.)

Jacinto stood tall and smacked his lips. "You know damn well who I'm talking 'bout. And now we know why you dragged us out here. Let me guess. She is going to be at this party?"

"Dammmn. Now I see why they call it Thirsty Thursday," Arismeldy said.

Mannn, fuck them. And Jacinto was wrong for swiping YES. But why was she on a dating app? She knew I existed. She knew my mack had no quit. She knew I had to drag my friends out there so that I could pretend that fate had us bump into each other at a frat party that I knew she was gonna be at, according to her IG post. A sign from the cosmos. Mercury retrograde telling us to go back to early summer when we were feeling each other, heavy-heavy. But this time I was gonna be more hood, like she wanted.

"Says on her profile that she's been a member since the summer." Jacinto patted my back. "Sorry, kid. Looks like it was a hot girl summer. And now it's a pantie-falling fall. *Nawww mean?*" He said it in my voice.

"Get off me." I shrugged his paw off my back. He was talking wild. She probably just forgot to deactivate the account. Or perhaps she left it there on purpose so that I would find it and get jealous. You know how they be with the cat and mouse games. And although I didn't even know Bethany's favorite color or movie, I knew enough.

Girls on the block be fiending for two-hundred dollar dates and bags with weird names like Hermès Birkin. You know. Shit my broke ass can't afford. Bethany, though, asked for nada. Then there was the time she said there was nothing a man could give her that she couldn't give herself. Which is true. Her pops gives her thousand-dollar allowances. And that's why it felt like a slap in the face when I was informed about generational trauma.

"It's crazy how colonization still got a hold on you," Jacinto said nonchalantly, like it was something obvious. "Shit living rent-free in your subconscious."

It wasn't necessarily what he said, it was how he said it. Sounded too smart, which made me feel dumb. "Explain that," I said.

"Chill, stop pressin' me. Let me focus on the mission at hand." He brushed me off to continue lurking for three girls.

Arismeldy laughed his ass off. So now I was feeling dumb-and-dumber; which translates to even more self-conscious. "Yo, that's the smartest shit I've ever heard Ja' say. You always chasing the snow bunnies. Dique, mejorando la raza." Arismeldy chuckled. "Sounds like you dying for your pops to live vicariously through you."

I couldn't help but chuckle too, because the other day, my father told me he saw a few snowflakes walking past the bodega. But Arismeldy and Jacinto were wildin'. If I like white girls so much, then why I date la loca Sofia for two years?

They told me she was Argentinean. A white person that speaks Spanish. Then Jacinto said some more smart shit. "Sofia was probably German."

Did you know that a bunch of Nazi goons escaped to Argentina after World War II?

That fact had Arismeldy stumbling around like there was an earthquake tickling him. He just kept laughing and laughing and stumbling around. "Jacinto! Who are you!?"

And Jacinto kept acting hella cool. "I don't know what you're talking about. I'm just your everyday sucio." He locked onto two girls walking. "Shit. Only two of them."

So now I'm feeling like the biggest dummie in the crew, which is ass because I'm the clique commander. *I* do the clowning. Yet I was still confused. "So Sofia was a Nazi?"

"No. Just saying that speaking Spanish doesn't make someone not white," Jacinto said.

"Aight, bet. I also dated—"

"Nathhhhhhalie," Arismeldy hissed. "She was Spaniard. A Spanish-speaking European. You like the white girls, bro. It'll be easier if you just admit it."

Let's just say that's true. I like white girls. Ain't nothing wrong with that, right?

"What's wrong is that you dragged us out here to—"

A loud raucous from the frat house pumped louder and louder. "Chug, chug, chug, chug! YYYEEEEEAAAAAHH!" All types of crazy, white-boy noises was coming out of there. No lie, sounded scarier than what I imagine a Young Republican rally would be like. Had us worried. Which was perfect. I wanted to escape that convo and situation all together. Leaving was a way to prove that I was not obsessed with the non-melanins. Lucky for me, I wasn't the only one.

"Bro," Arismeldy made hard eye-contact with me, "let's be out. I heard Tommy in Union City got open-cribs. If we leave now, we'd get here by 11."

"Na, yo! Let's go get one of those Fat Sandwich joints," Jacinto suggested.

And that's when we opened the two-liter Coke with the Bruggie, 'cause the night was definitely not over.

We pulled up to one of the Fat Sandwich spots. And I'll

admit, this bodega needs to step its game up because those sandwiches were on a different tier. (Yeah, yeah, yeah, if that's the case, why am I here making a sandwich? You got me there.)

"Pass the ketchup, bitch," Jacinto said as he reached across the wobbly table.

"Get your own, hoe," Arismeldy replied as he snatched the ketchup bottle out of Jacinto's reach.

"Whatchu call me?" Jacinto stood up.

Same bickering as before. But this time, I didn't bother to get between them. They all bark anyway. At most, they was gonna slap box until one of them complained that the other was playing too rough. That's when the bickering would start all over again. It's their…love language. Which is another thing I wanted to ask you. What do you know about love languages? That night, I asked Arismeldy and Jacinto the same question.

"It got something to do with communication," Jacinto said as he mauled through his Fat Sandwich with fries and mozzarella sticks dangling out of the bread.

"Thinking 'bout them book suggestions, I see," Arismeldy said. "Keeping it real, I mean, y'all know. I'm not your typical gay guy. I'm hella into sports, I dress straighter than most Dominican men—especially the ones that wear licria—and I don't have a gazillion girl friends. Like Yo! I'm a straight gay-guy. That statement doesn't even make sense, but it does. I'm a straight guy that isn't attracted to women. Ain't that some shit!?"

He had a point. The only way you'd know he's gay is if he told you. Dude can deadass get away with saying no-homo, like in high school, when guys would play chicken by inching their lips closer and closer to each other before one swerved away. (Arismeldy was the champ at that. What a savage.)

"So if we talking about those book recommendations, I think that self-love one is for me. Because sometimes I think I'm not really meant to be gay. And if I think that, how could I love myself?"

"It's called masturbation. La paja," Jacinto blurted out. His eyes trailed the butts of three girls that walked in.

"Ignore him," I said. "And daamn, bro. That was mad deep. I hope you not thinking of suicide or something." I said it just like that. Suicide or something. Like suicide is just something. But I've noticed how Arismeldy be full of life some days and full of…nothing, the next.

"Calm down, wierdo. Self-reflection doesn't come with a side of suicidal ideation. I'm just saying that I spend energy wrestling with questions like, Why don't I have gay friends? Am I really gay? Existential crisis is my norm. Like, what the heck am I really doing here?"

All facts. I was starting to ask myself those questions too. We were deadass an hour away from home, eating sandwiches, figuring out how to herd nine girls, just so I could win over some *other* girl that denied me the cheeks already. Is that life? Yo, it's that generational trauma I was talking 'bout. That mujeriego trauma. (Write that shit down 'cause I'mma make that word hot, watch.) Yet, leave it up to Jacinto to ruin the moment of reflection.

"Life is a simulation. Just not one as lit as *The Matrix*," Jacinto said. Again with that nonchalantness. He returned to making love to his sandwich.

"Shut the fuck up," me and Arismeldy said in unison.

"Good luck shutting me up. I spy three Betty-Boops looking this way."

Bruh…I should've never turned my head. I didn't catch much, but I caught enough melanin on them.

"Chill out, bro," Jacinto whispered. "You mad obvious."

"Aight, so wassup?" I said, energized by the prospect. Completely forgetting the conversation we were just having. If Bethany was too white, these mamis were everything else.

"They been sneaking glances this way. So you already know I forced eye contact with the one I call dibs on. The short, curly-haired one. Oh yeah, that's mine." Jacinto licked his lips. "The one that looks like the group cock-block is Arismeldy's. And Rico's is hand-selected by me. She morenita with dimples. She gonna be his gateway drug back into tubis and dark nipples."

I mean, that was a wild statement but after they riled me up about liking white girls too much, I didn't care. I stood up like Captain America and did what I do best: make moves.

"You just want fries, right?" I said with extra volume. Before they could answer, I said, "Aight, bet."

I stepped towards the counter with swag. My excuse to peep the mamis in incognito mode.

Curly had a Colgate smile. Her nose twinkled a bit with it. I could see why Jacinto called dibs on her with his #1 overall draft pick. My shortie, though? I couldn't see the morenita's face, but EL PIPO! Her thigh bookmarked the end of their table. A lap that said, Ho-Ho-Ho, Merry Thickmess if you sat on it. Un jamon bien sazonado. No exaggeration. And no, she wasn't fat; she was thick-thick. The type of thick that I had to second guess if I could even handle all that. But you know me, I'm all about the sí se puede.

"How can I help you, my friend?" an employee said.

I froze. Didn't expect Habibi to pull up to the register that quick. You know, I was just trying to check out the mamis. So I pretended to read the menu that was overhead, knowing damn well I wasn't going to order anything. After a few seconds, I pretended to be indecisive and pimp-walked back towards our table. The girls giggled as I passed.

"I'm game," I declared to Arismeldy and Jacinto.

"Oh, shit. They coming our way."

Arismeldy's girl, the presumed Secretary of Cock-Block Defense, led the way. "Hey, were you guys standing outside of the Gamma Pi frat house earlier?" she said.

Possibly. I never bothered to translate the Greek letters. But if we said we didn't know the letters, then it would've been a dead giveaway that we didn't go there.

"And if we were?" Arismeldy said. And that's the great

thing about him. Even though he gay, dude just likes to flirt. But he caught them a bit off guard. So I dunked his alley-oop.

"What he meant to say was, are you ladies trying to come with?"

"Gamma Pi, Gamma Thigh, it don't matter. We'll take you wherever y'all want," Jacinto wing-manned. He winked at the one he called dibs on too. Thought he ruined it for us, but they laughed at his antics.

"Y'all funny. But yeah, you read our minds. We are totally down." She glanced at her two friends for approval. They both nodded in agreement. "Okay, it's settled."

"What about the ratio?" Arismeldy said into my ear.

At that point, it was fuck the ratio. If we didn't get in, we didn't get in. I was dead set on going wherever these melanin-mamis took us.

Those girls were hella friendly on our walk to the frat house. They had their own bottle of Tito's and OJ that we helped gulp down. They were so comfy with us that the morenita swooped her arm under mine and clutched me close like a purse. I didn't give a rat's ass about Bethany anymore. Plus, I'd be a sucker to fumble—what at the moment seemed like an easy lay—for a hard-to-get Bethany.

"This is it!" morenita said. I think her name was Lorena, but I was distracted the whole walk there. Kept conjuring gay shit in my head in order to prevent a boner. Yo, I felt her thighs thundering the whole walk. Had me back to animal instincts.

(What? You still don't believe me? Bro, I swear on Juan Pablo Duarte that Shaquille O'Neal would need both hands to palm one cheek. You know what, I don't care if you think I'm exaggerating. It's my story.)

"You sure this the house?" I asked, 'cause I swore we had another block to go. But then again, we took another way there. This was the back route, I assumed.

Lorena—we just gonna say that's her name—playfully slapped my shoulder. "Of course it is. Says Gamma Pi right there." She pointed at massive Greek letters: an upside down L and the pi symbol from Algebra.

"Oh yeaaaah. This is it," I lied. Didn't matter, right?

Nope. It fucking mattered.

"Let's all take a shot before we go in and split off," Lorena suggested. Which was an odd thing to say, but I thought I was catching onto something. Thought she was trying to commandeer our own dark corner once inside. Perreo in our own esquina. Our rinconcito de travesuuurrrra. And I liked that idea. "Let's do it!" I said. I snuck in a whisper into Arismeldy's ear, "These college hunnies are *indeed* a different breed...bitch-ass hater." Thought I made him eat his words.

We cyphered the bottle of Tito's and OJ—as well as the Bruggie and Coke—around the circle, then galloped up the frat house steps. The brodie at the door did a quick headcount and said, "Y'all good to go. Jungle Juice is in the basement. Pong on the first floor. Second and Third floors are off-limits."

Three-to-one ratio, my ass! I thought. Let's gooooo! We in! Finna be a movie! My heart rate picked up past the point where the treadmill starts beeping. Could've been the liq kicking in or just excitement. Never been inside a frat house before, and we was bien acompañado. Thought dudes were gonna hate on us when they saw us squadded up with these mamis. HA-HA! *Annnd* they was playing Bad Bunny too. I dance-walked in. "Bad Bunny bebé-be-be." I smiled at Lorena, gave subtle we-did-it nods to Arismeldy and Jacinto. Ohhh the stories we were gonna tell the next morning. They were gonna go something like this:

Ayo, so this shortie that had been dripping me for weeks invited us to this frat house. So me and the crew, Arismeldy and Jacinto, went out there. Shortie started playing hard to get. Was about to flake on us. So you know me. I rallied up. Braveheart. Spit a little Cupido into these three mamis' ears. And when I say, mamis, I mean, you'd think they all got BBLs. Then we went to the frat house. Gamma Pi. Greek shit, you know. But not real Greek shit. The guy at the door hit us with a three-to-one ratio. We said, "Naw, B. Our mamis count for three each." They checked them out and said, "You right." Boom, we was inside. And when inside…

Bro, but when we got inside…

When. We. Got. Inside. "What the fuck?" snuck out of my lips.

"Yo!" I looked at Arismeldy and Jacinto. "What's with all the rainbow flags?" I looked over at the beer pong game to our right. "And what's with the shirtless dudes? And the dudes in the corner kissing each other?"

Lorena and her two girls jumped in front of us. "Thanks for getting us inside. Let's go girls! No circle of death tonight!" They danced away into the basement.

Jacinto squinted at a banner hanging on the staircase next to the pong game. "Gamma Pi. Gay Pride Fraternity Incorporated," he whispered, but I read his lips. "What y'all think that means?"

Arismeldy laughed. "It means it's finally y'all turn to wingman! The night is young!"

STROBERI

Rico sliced his sandwich in half and ate as he talked. "Shit had me—thinking a lot, cuzzo. Like—I literally played myself, naw mean?"

I swore I heard him say he got tricked into that frat house. In any case, this story is light compared to Yoskar's. "How so?"

"I ordered a couple of those books that the first shortie recommended on Amazon—which came in three days, not two." Rico shakes his head. "The reason I played myself was because of my own perspective. I assumed those girls were flirting with us because I'm fly, they fly, we matched. But they were just friendly. I also assumed all frats were—I don't know—straight, because I didn't think a gay frat was in the realm of possibility. Basically, the whole night and my whole life, I've been assuming that everything is a space for me. The wildest part, I never really thought about the homie, Arismeldy. He's always wingman-ing for us. Actively participating in Jacinto and I's sucio ways. Before that night, we've never done that for him. And I read that that could be because Arismeldy thought like us too. That all spaces were for straight men. So doing straight shit was his way of participating."

"Hold up. You learned all this from one party at Rutgers and reading a book?" I question. "And no disrespect, you read the whole book too? Past the table of contents?"

"Yeah, man. These books be explaining everything. Giving examples and stuff. It's like it got all the information that I never knew I needed." Rico takes out a book that he apparently had tucked in his lower back, against his belt. "Still couldn't let the hood see me with a book though, naw mean? Gotta keep my rep' intact."

I toss the sweaty book onto the sandwich counter.

"Wanna hear something crazier? We stayed at that party and still had a good time. Like, bro. Me and Jacinto having a blast at a gay frat house. Can you believe that?"

Even thinking about Arismeldy having fun at a gay frat house sounds like a stretch. I be forgetting he's gay some-times. "I don't know, man. 'Fun at a gay frat house' sounds very sus. You sure you don't got something else to tell me? I won't tell anyone, I promise."

"Stop plaaayyyying, bro! But, yo! That's the generational trauma I'm talking 'bout. Remember when you got into that wild car accident? You was shook to drive for a solid year. My theory is someone back-back in the day with power and influence had an awful experience with a gay dude. Let's just say the dick was wack. Left powerful dude underwhelmed or con el culo hinchado. He then went on to create homophobia. After, he passed homophobia down to his seeds. Same way racism got my dad and *then* me to like white girls without knowing. I'm just saying." Rico tosses his hands up. "Men have nipples."

"What!?"

"Us men have nipples. We are basically all women before we turn man. Google it. We learn sexism. Boom! Generational trauma." Rico explodes his fist near his temple. "Mind-blowing shit right there."

"Na, the only thing mind-blowing is you jumping all over the place with these wild examples. I think you need to be the student a little longer before becoming the teacher. And by a little, I mean a hot-minute."

"Read the book then, bitch." He shoves the book into my chest.

"And cut!" the cameraman says out of left field.

"Great work, guys," Carla, the reporter, says. "If Pelao Jr can be a little more confrontational, it would make a gigantic difference. People like to see drama unfold. The potential of fists flying and—"

"Whoa-whoa-whoa. Y'all can't be serious. You filmed all that?" I say, unaware of the camera the whole time. "I'm gonna need that footage before I figure out how to sue the station.”

“How does five-thousand sound?” she counters, handing me the papers.

“Where do I sign?”

The Bodega Kardashians II

STROBERI

The bodega on TV, Pops would have been hyped. Especially with the money they throwing my way. Which is an unsolved mystery. Why the heck would someone pay for this? I literally stand behind this counter, rando customers who think I'm their best friend come in and say random shit (half the time they lie). Confiding in me like I care. Sometimes they don't even buy anything, or *won't* buy anything unless it's "fiao". Then you got the regulars, like Rico, who come in and also don't buy anything. And there aren't even enough vecinos left to provide the real bodega experience.

I look outside towards the new condominiums. A young guy with a suit-sneaker combo rushes out of it and hops on NJ Transit to NYC.

Back in the day, that guy would have got roasted ten times before he got on that bus. I can hear the jokes now. *I see Justin Timberlake bye-bye-byed his way to the hood. McNerd (McNair) High School is the other way, bruh.*

I never even answered the reporter's initial questions. Specifically, why are we the last bodega in Jersey City? I guess my Pops's stubbornness colliding with his ignorance led to this. Even at that, I still gotta hand it to the man. Because of him, I've inherited a TV special! Yet, that weird feeling from before lingers. Something doesn't feel right. Am I stealing my father's fifteen-minutes? Am I honoring the community?

And speaking of fifteen minutes, after signing the day-long contract, that's how long it took the news station to roll up an extra van full of equipment. Transformed the bodega into a mini Best Buy: electronics everywhere, cameras in every corner, mics hidden in the shelving. They even hooked a GoPro onto G-Hombre's back. Their goal is to capture the stories and interactions inside of the bodega. And from here on out, every customer that walks out is given a disclosure statement and the choice to be blurred out on TV.

I'm souped. Hyped. Activo. This is surreal. Feels like I'm on the set of the first and last episode of an iconic sitcom. *The Fresh Prince of Bel Air* or *The Martin Show*. This actually feels like I'm living!

"Yo, yo, yo, yo. I'm back!" Rico announces his presence. He lifts a foot onto the counter in a hamstring stretch. "Had to whip out the Butters. Unlaced like a loose straight-jacket, naw mean? Classic joints. Gonna teach that Carla news-reporter-lady about knocking boots. What you think? When I'm laid up on her bed, should I keep a Timb' on or naw?"

This guy. I don't think he knows they recording yet. I should save him, but na. Nobody told him to walk in this reckless (again). (Maybe observing self-sabotage is fun.) "You know she white, right?" This will give the audience a laugh.

Rico closes his eyes and slowly cocks his head back, charging up his rage, "COÑÑÑO. You're fucking right. Damn, son. They really out here trying to keep me traumatized. Disengaged from reality. But yo, check it. What if she hollas at me? That wouldn't be mejorando la raza. That would be me taking the handout. Free coochie like it's free lunch."

"Free coochie is dirty coochie. Same way your dick is dirty dick. Same way free school lunch was always ass except for Fridays. Nothing free of effort is ever worth having."

"Fuck outta here, son. I get tested all the time. But did you read the book?"

It's been less than half an hour since he handed it to me, how he expect me to have read it? "Yeah, I read it."

"So how you like it?"

"My favorite part was making sure I didn't crease the binding. You know, like how you don't like to crease your sneaks."

"Ahhh, you didn't read shit." He wags his finger at me. "Where Carla at, though? I'm trying to get my followers up on social media. I don't know if you know, but that's the new car."

Before I can even question his statement, he continues.

"Ten years ago, if you had no whip, you got no chick. Now it's, if you got no followers, you got no swallowers. Naw mean?"

Gross, but I actually do understand what this clown is saying. Attention is the latest form of currency, after crypto. And attention from a popular person is worth the most.

"Yoooooooo. Just thought about something. What if white dudes got the same generational trauma that I got for the snow bunnies? But they got it for that Latin fever. Remember Perico Pin-Pin?"

"The salsa?"

"Na, not the song. Well, he got his name from the song but I'm talking 'bout the salsa instructor. El blanquito viejo, who always strutting his moves. The one that is always saying shit like Suzie-Q and Copa."

"Oh, yeaaaaah. The crazy white dude that harasses all the Latinas on the block. What about him?"

"He got a villain origin story." Rico leans in closer and whispers, "Mamaguebo. Just peeped the camera on the side and the mic behind the plátanos. Why didn't you tell me anything?"

I toss my hands in the air. *"Bueeeno."* The Dominican way of saying, *I mean*…got nothing to do with me. "But yo, let me holla at you in the bathroom real quick."

The door chimes, announcing a customer.

"Oh snap, it's the OG, Ramon!" Rico changes focus. His annoyed facial expression quickly turns into a smile.

"Finally, that old man owes me money."

The old man of at least eighty years waddles into the store. Harmless, as always.

"Cómo estás, Ramon? Y la familia?" Rico welcomes OG Ramon into the store.

"Ahí en la lucha. Oye, ustedes conocen a Joselito? Que vi que anda por ahí."

Me and Rico look at each other. "No. We don't think so."

"No, tú lo conoces. Yo se que tú lo conoces."

"Joselito...?" I look at Rico for a hint.

"Sí, ese mismo."

"Joselito…quién sera?" I question again.

"Pero amigo, tú conoces a Joselito," he says with a serious look. After a brief pause, he says, "El quién te rompió el culito." He busts out in laughter.

I smack my lips in annoyance, but that was so random that I quickly laugh too. "Ramon, ju funny mi friend." I attempt to match Ramon's broken English, which he occasionally showcases. "Pero help me out real quick. I need to talk to Rico in private, so hold the store down for a bit."

"Ju hurry up con prisa. I work por minuto." Ramon parks himself in front of the counter, safekeeping the cash register. Although he's a mala-paga, I can always trust him to watch the store for a few minutes.

I pull Rico into the bathroom, away from the cameras and mics.

"Yo, bro, I think we can use this situation to actually do good." Pops said to serve the community, so I'mma honor that on the last day. "If we continue with this passive recording of bodega life, we just gonna get a bunch of dudes coming in here talking nonsense."

"My fault, bitch," Rico says, offended. "How was I supposed to know?"

"It's all good. Your arrival literally got us this TV deal, so the ends justify the means in your case. But now that we got the cameras on us, I'mma need your help."

"Anything you need."

"That's what I'm talking 'bout." I pound his chest. My cousin Rico may be ridiculous at times but he always looking out. "One, we need to get the old neighborhood back in here. Can you handle that?"

"Too easy. I'll just tell them the aguacates are half off. Cool?"

I mean, it's the bodega's last day—even though they don't know that, Rico either. "Sure."

"What else you need?"

"Second, let's get women in here to tell their stories."

"Come on, son. You already know nobody sends their daughters or sisters to the bodega. Half the time they only come in here to hide from catcallers."

"I said women, not teenaged girls. And who you telling? I work here. That's the whole point of me bringing this up. Let's get some women in here. Tell them they gonna be on TV, if need be," I say. "And please don't just get girls that you trying to bag." I look him dead in the eye, making sure my point gets across.

"Na, man. I'm on a new path of enlightenment. Just a

little mixed up internally. Do I bag shorties or do I not bag shorties? I don't know. Everything sounds like it could be generational trauma and—"

"Rico, chill out. Not that deep. Just hit up the old vecinos so we can make the bodega's corner look less like a breeding ground for sexual harassment." I glance outside. Three middle-aged men with beer bellies just there posted-up watching girls walk by. Later they'll start playing bachata, whip out the Styrofoam cups, and maybe play dominoes.

"Say less." Rico gives an evil smirk. "You know what I'm thinking?"

"Damn, I think I do." I scratch my head in contemplation. Rico is gonna get Las Mamis in here. A group of local women that recite poetry, spoken word, and anything pro-feminism, pro-Afro-Latinidad. It would have been my first idea too, but they are known to get a little…unconventional. Like the one time they stormed the corner with picket signs and loudspeakers, protesting catcallers by catcalling men. The image of Mira, the ringleader, saying, "*Dammmn*, Papi. You giving little dick energy, but I can work with anything," to Rico lives rent free in my mind. I fucking cried laughing. Yeah, we can definitely use Las Mamis. "Fuck it, do it. Tell them that now that we have cameras on us, let's show the world that the hood is not an episode of *Gangland* or *Bait Car*. It's a place of artistic expression and intellectuals discourse too. Let's show them that the bodega is not just where you go for a four-dollar ham and cheese, catch up on the local chisme headlines, and find that one person that been ducking you for weeks; this is also a place that connects the whole block together. So get them here. In the mean time, I'll have OG Ramon keep the cameras rolling."

"You sure about that? OG Ramon came in here with that random-ass slander. He got us looking like the neighborhood Booty Goons."

That's true, OG Ramon came in here talking wild. "I'll tell one of my stories then. Just get Las Mamis here on the double."

"You a wild man." Rico chuckles. "If I'm not back in twenty minutes, assume they kidnapped me. A'ight?"

"I gotchu."

Rico half jogs out of the bodega.

"Ramon, ju funny guy, well I'm funny guy too. Let me tell you a story that you won't necessarily understand, but needs to be said out loud."

Ramon shrugs a I-have-no-clue-what-ju-just-said, but I continue anyway.

STROBERI'S CAPICÚA

STROBERI

You're at the dominoes table cheesing hard as hell because you're about to slam your uncles with a capicúa, when suddenly, it hits you. You've deadass wasted the last five hours playing dominoes with a bunch of fifty-year-olds that wouldn't stop asking you, Cuántas novias tienes, until you lied and said two.

Five hours.

Ten uncles.

Twenty variations of the same question:

Cuántas jevas?

Cuántas amiguitas?

Y la otra? Y *las* otras?

Y las gringas que van para tu escuela?

You don't bother to say you graduated high school two years ago because the previous five times you told them this didn't seem to drill that information into their heads. But you find consolation in the fact that they've stopped asking about her.

Her.

It's not that you've forgotten her name like your uncles forgot your replies. You're just dedicated to the Harry Potter route by refusing to say it. And you're okay with that. Even though every time you say, Her, the name Angelica lights up behind your forehead. So you decide to pound a few brews, your attempt at washing her name off, when on beer six, a sudden jolt of a-lo-foke tilts your beer up into a chug. And once you down it you glance at your uncles thinking they actually do got a point. Where the fuck are my bitches? I'm too young to have no hoes. So you text your boy, Zeke Nasty, with a, Where the bitches at, and he promptly replies, Say less my guy. Slide through.

He replied so fast that you assume he had been waiting all day for your text, so now you hyped thinking he got a surplus of hoes that he needs help with. Unfortunately, when you do show up, it's just him and Jacinto in the dusty ass basement watching *Love is Blind*.

What's your next move? 'Cause it's definitely not to call it a night. Instead, you make yourself at home and pour yourself whatever concoction Zeke Nasty got in the cranberry juice bottle that looks more like grapefruit now. And oh boy does it taste amargo. Fitting for the amargue you suffer for Her.

After a second cup, Zeke Nasty launches off the beat-up couch and says, Ronnie got open-cribs!

You wanna look him in the eye and say, it's about damn time, but her name blinds you now. You can barely think of anything but Her.

But you're committed to your goal of sliding into something warm and wet tonight, so you go to that party. And when you arrive, you have no inhibitions left. You're pressed against the sweaty wall with a red Solo cup full of whatever-gets-the-job-done, while a sucia rubs her sundress into you, and it feels good. You feel like a man. But you still want it to feel better, so you try your best to align your dick with her crack, just so you can feel the cheeks clap a little more, but the song changes to Bad Bunny and the image of him in the "Yo Perreo Sola" music video jumps at you. Now you think the shortie in front of you is a dude in a wig and the barf that launches out of you is all over shortie's back.

So what do you do now that her screams of disgust are muting out the music? Do you help her? Do you apologize? Do you continue smearing the vomit on her back in your failed attempts to wipe it off?

Nope.

You just continue singing the lyrics to the song, que ningún baboso se le pegueeee, until the Vomit Scream-Queen calls for her older brother that looks like he spent a few months in juvie. You know you not the toughest guy, but you know if you gonna get stomped out, you'll at least get in a hit or two. But you bonkers off the jungle juice and coordination isn't your thing right now. So you stumble through the crowded basement while the older brother figures out what happened to his sister. He gives chase, but by the time he does, you already double-stepping it up the stairs. And little do you know, those stairs lead to hell. But don't worry, you won't reach hell just yet. Although it may feel like it.

Your heart rate has kicked up. And the jungle juice is white river rafting through your bloodstream, making you drunker and drunker. At this point, you're all about Jesus take the wheel and you're hoping Jesus isn't white because that would mean he has a moderate probability of being racist so you hope someone else takes the wheel if that's the case.

And then that's when you burst into the laundry room thinking it was the front door. There you meet una diabla. (Because of the impending awful experience, you take this encounter as confirmation that Jesus is indeed Deep-South Alabama white…and racist.) A cutie with a youthful smile that shines even brighter than Angelica's name (that fixated itself behind your forehead after drink seven). You question what she's doing there, so she crushes a pill on top of the dryer and offers you a hit. You don't question it. You don't question anything anymore. A few moments later, you realize that you are sober now. The drugs counteracted the alcohol. But your body is so mixed up with chemicals and emotions that your brain records her face as sobering you. She brought clarity to you. She is love. She is the one. Your brain releases endorphins every time you see her, and you see a lot of her. A summer's worth to be exact (twenty years if we consider how slow a summer in hell would feel like).

Oh wait, that summer of hell had been repeating in a loop, over and over, because you couldn't wake up from la maldita drug-induced coma you fell into that night.

So you're in this coma, but you can still hear people from time to time. Your family visits you regularly at the hospital and the uncles that refuse to go to church come in and use you as confession. One uncle confides that he has a little dick and that has led him to become a habitual liar in front of his friends. They've even nicknamed him Mandingo after all the times he's stuffed his jeans with a plátano. Another uncle tells you he cheats on his wife because he feels small next to such a strong woman. Cheating is his way of feeling like a strong man. And the last one that stopped by. The. Last. One. Said he can't stop glancing at his teenage nieces' asses. So that slaps you awake, and you're awkwardly face to face with your uncle.

Does he know you heard him? Does he know you're about to hurt him? You're about to pop off on him when you notice your arms had gotten deflated as fuck in those bedridden three months. So you uncock your Jell-O of a fist with great timing because your uncle shouts, Pero Muchacho! Before calling out, Martína (your mother's name)! Your mom rushes in and behind her, just as fast, is Her. Angelica.

Your mom tells you that you've been KO'ed all summer but only after asking you, Pa eso es que tú bebe? A question that never begs to be asked, especially when she needs to tell you that in those three months, your Pops passed away from cirrhosis and now you gotta manage the bodega.

Angelica tells you that she is glad you're awake because she had been waiting to release a punch-to-the-balls worth of guilt. I had sex with Zeke Nasty, she said, followed by another gut wrench, while we dated.

You want to be mad, especially because you thought Zeke Nasty was your boy, but you've realized that you didn't just visualize Angelica's name in your head, you also just said it. So you take the scandalous news in stride because at this point, you don't give a fuck. You're just happy to be awake. Craving to live life. But here comes hell. La bodega. As if the bedridden coma wasn't enough. Now you're stuck behind a cash register for sixteen hours a day, seven days a week. Over and over. Until…

You, become the twenty-year-old protagonist to a TV news special! Let's get it! We live baby! From the last bodega in Jersey!

(Oh, shit! I see Las Mamis pulling up now. "Ramon, hide!")

PART II:
LAS MAMIS

Claribel's Top 5 Questions

Why Do Straight (Dominican) Men Wear Tight Jeans?

No woman knows.

Perhaps it's 'cause they want you to look at their plátano…or guineito? The imprint of it sloping down their thigh makes them feel sexy. Doubly serving as their mating call. Triply serving as their way of showing confidence.

Perhaps it's because women's clothing cost less. And those are the tightest jeans they can buy. A rare convergence between high quality and low price.

Perhaps they have too many girl siblings. And the age gap was so close that the hand-me-downs were unisex.

Perhaps they like feeling saran-wrapped. Compensating for the hugs their fathers never gave them. Or the hugs they never gave themselves. The jeans prescribed by the local brujx to keep their inner demons sealed tight.

And what if one of those demons snuck out? The one that wants to whisper into every girl's ear. The one that told them, "Forgo the men's section and go to the women's because that's where the mamis are at."

Perhaps they are gay? Or non-binary? Or simply like the fabric. The softness. The elasticity. A euphemism for their equally tender inner-self; a blatant hint of femininity showcasing their masculinity is secured.

Really…no woman knows.

Maybe I'm looking too into something that is circumstantial. Or easily defined as an act of spontaneity. Who knows? Could have been a mistake turned into an addiction. Like my dumbass who dated Pablo, a man-child cloaked in a facade of fidelity, who happened to wear tight jeans. Which leads me to my next question.

Why do *I* like men who wear tight jeans? (That shit isn't even cute.)

I may never know.

But those men must be stopped.

Where Did You Find That New Chisme?

Did you dream it?

Did you give un mal de ojo so fierce that you manifested it?

Porque, diablo! You knew about the chisme before me, and the chisme was *about* me!

So dime...where did you hear that chisme?

Because you didn't hear it from me.

My mother, perhaps?

El vecino put an ear to the wall?

La vieja brechadora, who doesn't know how to use WhatsApp, te lo gritó from her balcón?

Dime, where?

Because while I was cagando, wiping my butt, my primo texted me saying, "Oye, dique tú fumigaste el edificio entero con tu churria."

And when I asked him who told him, he said you.

So dime...como tú supiste?

I'm not calling you a liar. You spoke the truth. But how did you know?

I put the chain lock on la puerta.

I sprayed Poo-Pourri.

Hasta le eche Mistolín.

So dime...

Ohhhhhhhhh, so that's how you knew.

El Grupo de WhatsApp.

When Did White, Christian Men Decide That My Titties Are for Sex and Not for Breastfeeding?

I wasn't going to ask, but I just saw homeboy across the street walking without a shirt.

It's hot outside. I get it. Like I, *get-it* get-it.

I'd love to toss this bra off and walk around puti-suelta to avoid this boob sweat too.

But nooooooooo, some clowns decided that my titties are for sex, and male titties are for…who the fuck knows?

And if my titties aren't for breastfeeding, since everyone is appalled by a breastfeeding mother, what the heck are my titties for then?

Look-look-look! See homeboy crossing the street? Them shits are flapping. He got more titty than me!

Damn. Why are white Christian-Mingle-ass-men so aggy?

Who Convinced Men That Catcalling Was the Way to a Woman's Heart?

It is literally the least effective way. Punto y aparte.

(Do I really gotta say more?)

Why Don't the Cops Pull Over Men in Gray Sweatpants for Indecent Exposure?

Gray sweats is male lingerie.

The butt is jiggling.

The bulge is hollering for attention.

And it's not just saying, "Psss-psss. Look at me."

It's saying, "You like dick? 'Cause I GOT dick."

It's saying, "I know you a good girl, but we all got nasty thoughts.

It's saying, "Give me a motha'-fuckin' traffic citation, because I'm your next accident, mami chula."

It's sorcery, I tell you! One that rivals that of Gandalf the Grey.

(I know I said I had five questions, but now I gotta ask 'cause I just got a paragraph from the *homie*, saying, "If you need anything. You know I'm here for you. And I mean anything ;-) Because a girl like you should have it all. Your ex, Flako, is ridiculous for doing you wrong. I swear some men ain't shit. But I'm here for you.)

Why Do People Claim They're in the Friend Zone?

A friend supports.

A friend listens.

A friend cares.

A friend communicates.

A friend tells you how it is.

A friend doesn't agree, just to agree.

A friend is there for the good times and the bad.

A friend is there during heartbreak,

during failure, during loss.

A friend lends a consoling hand…

…but not on your thigh.

(Like the *homie* did last night after I broke up with Flako —his first attempt at hollering.)

A friend doesn't do all of the above, secretly waiting to sex the other.

So why all these friend-zone victims *capping*? You can't be in the friend zone, if you were never a true friend to start with. So what they really in is the predatory long-con zone. Because no friend should wish for my relationships to fail, before sliding into my DMs.

Beatriz Plays
Never Have I Ever

Let's Play a Game of "Never Have I Ever"

You know how it goes. Make your hands visible and I'll say something I've never done before. If you've done it, lower a finger.

(1) Never have I ever laid hands on a girl's waist as I passed her, to then whisper, "Excuse me."

(2) Never have I ever gone a week without being told I'm too pretty to not be smiling.

(3) Never have I ever been able to walk home at night without making makeshift brass-knuckles with my keys.

(4) Never have I ever had a handyman in my apartment without asking a male friend to come over.

(5) Never have I ever not inspected my drinks at a bar.

(6) Never have I ever been friendly without the fear of it being misinterpreted as flirting.

(7) Never have I ever been able to turn down a man's sexual advance without assessing the possibility of violence.

(8) Never have I ever group-chatted nudes sent to me in private.

(9) Never have I ever explored my sexuality without degrading myself as a hoe.

(10) Never have I ever been able to mind my own business—at the bus stop, the gym, the cafeteria—without being sexually harassed.

How many men still have a finger up?
Oh, you queer? My bad, my bad. Show off them fingers then!
For those with their fingers down, though…

**...punch yourself in
the face, with the
fists you've
just made.**

Borikisha's
Red Flags

BORIKISHA

Red Flag Number-One

He gave me the password to his phone without resistance. When I asked, I was just testing him; curious to see if he had any hood-ratas on his phone. So when he tapped it in in front of me, I thought it was sweet of him to reassure me. But I should have been suspicious. Because that was on our first date.

Red Flag Number-Two

My Pitbull kept sniffing him up and down. I just thought he was good with dogs. But now I know it was because he *is* a dog. And my Pit' was sniffing that perra—the one he was cheating on me with—on him.

Red Flag Number-Three

After every double he pulled at T-Mobile, he gave me BV. A coochie knows when it's getting cheated on.

And since you're laughing at his last antic, I know what type of person you are too. I ain't saying you a hoe, I'm just saying you support this nonsense. Don't roll your eyes at me! You probably think I'm the crazy one because I got a tubi on. But hear me out.

RED FLAG NUMBER-FOUR

He would get awkward around my Pops. And only around my Pops. Let me spell that out for you.

D   A   D   D   Y   -   I   S   S   U   E   S

How many more red flags did I need? Guess.

…

None.

(STROBERI! Get your ass out here and give me a fucking loosie on the house before I wreck this bodega. Because just saying this shit got me tight. He hands me the loosie. Now that's more like it. I light it and take a long drag. What? I can't smoke in here? Yeah, you THOUGHT. I'mma do lo que me de la maldita gana. I puff out an O.)

You see, I didn't need no more red flags because the next flag…the *next* flag…belonged on the Stonewall National Monument. Handstitched for June 28th. You get what I mean? A fucking rainbow flag. I saw him leaving Chicho Riso's crib one morning. Shirt unbuttoned.

Till this day, I don't know if he's a straight man who likes his booty hole licked or if he truly gay. I puff out a long drag. But…I'm not mad anymore. The new blanquitos on the block—bunch of George Michaels out here walking around, holding hands like it's Last Christmas—taught me something new about Latino men: Y'all so homophobic that you can't even be gay in peace.

Latino gays be on the low-low-low. Lower than a stripper dancing to Flo Rida. Ain't that wild? Let me dissect that. You see them small Mexican aguacates over there on the shelf next to the yuca? The black ones. How many times do Ricans and Domis come in here and complain about them? "Where the real aguacates at? Where the ones from our patios at?" Meanwhile, they basically the same shit! The blanquitos don't give a fuck, though. They buy all the aguacates they can press their thumb on. While the Domis and Boris are held back by the idea that aguacates that aren't from their islands aren't aguacates. And according to our norms, anything LGBTQ is a Mexican aguacate. So who am I to be mad at someone who lives mad at themselves? It would've just been redundant.

Silence was mi mayor venganza.

What? I should say something to him? Bitch, I didn't make the rules to machismo. Será yo tan importante. What you

think, I started that trend? That's somebody else's respon-
sibility. Because no señor. There are about four billion men
in this world and you want a woman to start solving shit?
Abusador del Diablo.

(Ayo, Stroberi, dame una cervecita. Don't play me. I know
all bodegueros be sipping on the low. I slide open the ice
cream freezer in front of the register. Damn, you wasn't
playing. You a sober hoe. But damn, he looking cute.)

(Chacho, Papi...*Arro', que carne hay!* When you taking me on
a date?)

(I'm not your type? How would you know that, if you've
never dated a gata like me?)

(You just know? Nobody *just* knows. Será tú Walter Mercado.
Shanti Ananda.)

(What if I rap for you a little? Oh, you smiling now. Say
less, Pelaito. My middle name is Maria by the way. So check
my flow.)

Maria, se fue. Maria is back!
Soy yo! Maria, la que se fue.
Where I've been, Where I've been at?
Don't worry about that!
Bonchinchero!
Presentao!
Just know I'm back with some facts.

Number one, la banda didn't play hasta la
quince.
I stopped that shit!
Even gave Solido a slap.
Because I won't be a Bebesita to a man like
that!

Un cuernu, un perro, not like Pelao,
Un hombre Stroberi,
yo quiero a mi la'o.

(So what's up? El anillo pa cuando?)

(WHOA! Who you talking to like that!? Dique I'm a whole
red flag, myself. No-no-no-no, nobody is moving too fast.
You just moving too slow. Whatever, I'm out of here. Your
loss.)

Mira Declares, Negrita Soy

MIRA

You tell me I can't celebrate my Blackness on Black History Month because my birth certificate says Honduras. Because the nationality on my passport says Honduran. Because, according to you, Black people don't speak Spanish.

Stop trying to hijack Black History Month.

Save your pride for Hispanic Heritage Month.

Like our ancestors didn't get shackled in the same West Africa that lies near the same Prime Meridian and Equator. Like they weren't transported on the same ten-ton Heskeths, Guineamens, and 566-ton Parrs. Like they weren't exposed to the same new world of disenfranchisement and neglect.

Wait...or were our ancestors Black Caribs? Interminglers turned Garífuna. I mean, we don't even know the specifics of our ancestral journey. If that isn't Black, then I don't know what is. But I'll keep entertaining you.

What if I stopped rolling my r's and claimed, This is America, we no speaky Spanish. Would you then consider me Black? I mean...I already look the part. The lips, the curves, the hair. If you didn't know me, wouldn't you just assume I was Black? The type of Black that you don't even bother to place to a country. Not Black from Ghana. Not Black from Haiti. Just Black.

If you dare say no, then mi querido primo, you a fucking liar. 'Cause you Black too. The same Black that adorned Celia Cruz's tumbao. The same Black that smacked Roberto Clemente's 3000 hits.

I get it primito. It's confusing. But when will you understand that the word, Honduras, doesn't describe me like the word, Black, does? That the word, Latino, is roughly two centuries old and accounts for a blip of our heritage. That the word, Hispanic, accounts for even less. That the word, Spanish, has more to do with Spain than it does with who we are.

Have you even read the history books!? I'm talkin' 'bout the real history books.

If you did, you'd claim your Blackness with the quickness. 'Cause I mean...like primo, our bloodline is amazing. We come from freedom fighters, abolishers of oppression, champions of the people. Why would I abandon that history? Why would I neglect it?

I speak English. So what? I speak Spanish. So what? Did I have a choice?

Wasn't our heritage taken from us?

STROBERI

Mira stares into the camera, then into the negro in my eyes. Before she can ask me if I'm Black—in which I'd likely acid reflexively say I'm Dominican—I blurt out, "Told you you was Black with a capital B," towards Rico.

"Hmm," Mira mums, turning to Rico.

Figured I'd divert the question to him because shieeeet, I know I'm Black but I gotta choose my battles wisely. This topic starts more arguments at the family barbeque than the drunk uncles at the dominoes table.

"And you's a Bitch with a capital Cardi B," Rico snaps back. "I ain't Mira's cousin! Joe Arroyo's 'Rebelion' and Maelo's 'Las Caras Lindas' my favorite salsa joints." Rico starts dancing in place.

"Oh, yeah?" I say. This clown lying on his dick, so I swiftly scroll through my pop's CD binder and find Ismael Rivera. I skip the tracks until "Las Caras Lindas".

"Ayyyyyyy!" Rico cries out, before dance-stepping towards Mira. He gently grabs her hands and sings, "Las caras lindas, las caras lindas, la cara linda de mi negriiiita, Mira!" He spins Mira and winks at me like he just bagged.

"You see these moves, Stroberi!?

"You see these hips!?

"I'm Black, Baby!"

...and I. AM. BLACK. TOO.

Part III:
The Ghetto
Rebellion

The Bodega Kardashians III

LA MUDA CARIÑOSA

"What up, Twitter Thumbs?" Stroberi says with his typical cheezy smile. He's a nice guy. Funny. And although that's the hundredth time he's called me that in an attempt to rile me up, I won't curse him out today. Instead, I'll just stick out my middle-finger.

"Dammmmmn. It's like that!?" His smile widens.

I stick out my other middle-finger now. Where the cameras at anyway? I got a story to tell. I look around the store, in between the isles. Fuck, Rico here too. If one wasn't enough.

"Ayo, Rico! Guess who's here?"

"Who-who-who?"

Rico curiously walks around from behind the deli counter. He takes one look at me and whiplashes his head back into a chicken-head neck roll. "Ohhhhhh shit! Miran quién e'. La tipa that always got something to say."

I sigh. They lucky they smile when they say this nonsense.

"Tell her to talk to me nice, though. She came in here middle-fingers blazin' like a Clint Eastwood Western," Stroberi says.

Aighhhhht. They clearly got the time to joke around today. I type away on my phone and send the message to Stroberi.

Maldito palomo how many times u gunna remind me that I'm mute?

"Alright, alright." He turns toward Rico. "She don't want that smoke today." And in the worst sign-language I've ever seen, Stroberi says, "You know we love you."

Rico in now the *new*, worst sign-language I've ever seen, says, "Yeah, and don't forget that!"

I'm taken aback. Wow. They took the time to learn my language. I feel warmth crawl up my body as my hand presses over my heart and my lips quiver with the rush of forming tears. I may just…cry.

Oh, hell no! I stick both middle-fingers up; one for each. And rush out of the store. Gangstas don't cry.

STROBERI

"Pelao Jr, can we talk outside?" Carla Rossi says. She stands at the entrance with her arms crossed.

For a second, my heart stops. Till I remember, Carla isn't my girlfriend, ex, or anyone I've messed around with lately. So it can't be one of *those* can-we-talks.

"Rico, handle the register."

"Tato. But when you get back, we gotta find out if Sammy Sosa technically still Black."

Outside the bodega a line has formed—longer than a Jordan release—of old vecinos trying to get on TV.

"De lo mío!" someone shouts, amongst the disorganized line.

"Pe-lao! Pe-lao! Pe-lao!" the line chants.

Ayyyy, people out here putting respect on my name! A smile sneaks out, but I quickly straighten my face and nonchalantly toss a peace sign their way. Gotta look cool about this all. Carla isn't impressed, though.

"Pelao Jr, those women said a lot." Carla exhales emphatically. "Like a lot a lot."

"I know, right? They really showed out. Said things that needed to be said. I can tell them to keep going if you want."

"No. Like I said, they said a lot. And it was great…but… it wasn't digestible."

"Huh?"

"Our audience likes things simple, in ways that they are accustomed to. Think headlines: FOUR ARRESTED IN

GREENVILLE DRUG RAID, GANG VIOLENCE KILLS THREE YOUTHS. You understand?"

"Not really. What does drugs and gang violence have to do with the bodega?"

"Exactly! That is why I've selected your next customer." Carla waves over a woman I've never seen before in my life. Dominicana for sure by the looks of her: Coco Chanel belt buckle on Bergenline jeans and Asian spa slippers. "This is Niña and her story is prime time."

Niña smirks like she got that good chisme. That I gotta pull over to the side of the road type of chisme. But what she gotta do with gangs, drugs, and the bodega? Something is a little off about this lady, too. One eye is looking directly at me, the other is twitching a bit like it's Morose-coding "K lo k".

Carla directs Niña toward the bodega entrance. "Thanks for understanding, Pelao Jr."

I don't understand jack-shit. But whatever. It's their show, anyway.

Niña Retells the Mal de Ojo Contagion of '96

NIÑA

You know, you would think that women dominate the cheffing field but they don't. It's men. Emeril Lagasse, Bobby Flay, Gordon Ramsay, Wolfgang Hockeypuck. Yeah, yeah, yeah, Rachel Ray exists, and I've heard Martha Stewart can make a beast weed-brownie. But have you ever watched Iron Chef? It's basically Ninja Warrior sautéed with random ingredients (see what I did there? I'm hilarious). It's hella mamaos up in that staged-kitchen.

So I'm here to state the obvious: most women cook at home, not restaurants.

Why? It's simple: men.

But not Dulce Linda la Leona.

Ohhhh, you never heard of her, right? Why would you? Giving her any type of shine would have crumbled the culinary world. Why? 'Cause chefs think that configuring a profitable recipe to be served 50 times a night is the ulti-mate form of cooking. They want you to believe that cooking should involve science at each step. Well tell that to Dulce Linda from the block. The same Dulce Linda that cooked a sancocho so good that she single-handedly cured the Mal De Ojo Contagion of '96.

Dammnnn, you don't know about the Mal de Ojo Contagion of '96, either? Y'all must be Gen-Z.

Ponte atento 'cause this story has many details and I don't like repeating myself to no one.

It started with the first luxury apartment building. The one next to Doña Chesca's crib.

Y'all don't know her, either? Do y'all even go here? Didn't y'all play outside growing up? Old lady is always on her balcony brechando.

Whatever. Just know that these people live on the block.

So those buildings were made to attract gentrifiers, of course. A beacon to call out the rich, white 27-year-olds from their parents' suburban basements. And you already know (or don't) nobody from here was gonna afford them. At least not at full price. Section 8, baby! The town had struck a deal with the management team. Build the apartments, but a quarter of the units had to be made available for Section 8 housing. So you best believe half the block jotted their name down on that waiting list.

We talkin' dishwashers, in-unit washer-dryers, central heating. No more gunshot-noises coming from the radiator and pipes. We talkin' things that we hardly knew existed.

For example, I bet you think a dishwasher is just a job title.

Na, it's also a machine! Put your tratos in there before bed and BAM! Next morning all clean. You best believe I also signed up. You'd be silly not to.

So everybody signed up, but since it was a lottery, not everyone got in. And everyone knew the process, so that didn't kickoff the Mal de Ojo Contagion of '96—yo, y'all probably don't even know what Mal de Ojo is. For starts, it ain't Bad Bunny's third eye. Mal de Ojo is Evil Eye.

Ahhhh, now y'all know what it is?

What? You only speak un po-qui-to Español?

First you don't play outside, second you don't wanna learn Spanish. Well I ain't conforming. Forget I even called it Evil Eye. Mal…de…O…Jo.

That's what everybody got after the lottery. Again, not because they didn't win the lottery, but what happened after. A few of the lucky families that got into the new apartments started stunting.

For context, in '96 the block was still Latino, 'cept for the few early gentrifiers. Yet, it looked like the Section 8 heads from the luxury apartments were gentrifying the block too. Beamers, Benz, and Teslas. Actually, maybe not Teslas, but you know I be media totada; I've been missing a screw since I fell down my steps a few years ago. In any case, they looked drug-dealer rich. Some of the girls got their bodies done in DR. Men started flexing thick Cuban-links. Yet, these were the same heads that would come to the bodega and swipe their EBT cards like it was an Amex

Black Card. I'm telling you, these were the type of people that would turn broke people into Republicans. 'Cause it's hard to bust your ass everyday working, to then see others living better by mooching off the government. Even if you know that it's only a few of them milking the system, it makes you think everyone on government aid is like that. So that's when the Mal de Ojo started. People who actually needed Section 8, and worked hard to get by, cursed those who were stuntin' with their government donations. They got that Evil Eye with the harshness. But it's not like the people giving Mal de Ojo knew what they were doing. Evil Eye just sorta happens. It is dark energy seeping out of negative emotions and malicious intent. So instead of cursing the flashy Section 8ers with poor health, bad luck, or money problems, they evil-eyed the groceries coming in and out of the bodega. The other Section 8ers in that building, the ones that were busting their asses working, also started giving Evil Eye to the flashy Section 8ers because they were now getting a bad rep too. Guilty by association. Then the dead-beat Section 8ers with the new cars started evil-eying the entire block because they claimed everyone was hating on them. It was a meeessssss. The Egyptian, Greek, and Mayan Gods of Evil Eye were working overtime. Until…yep…Dulce Linda came through with the sancocho of a lifetime.

Remember how I said the groceries coming out of the bodega were getting cursed? People were losing their appetite. Their food was tasting like a white Thanksgiving—no seasoning and lots of raisins—no matter how much seasoning they put on it.

It got so bad that the block was ready to file a class-action suit against Goya for what they believed to have been a change in the Adobo recipe. Badia Spices was up next for a lawsuit too. Listen, it was bad. Because during the 1990 economic recession, people gave up on warding evil. Nobody was wearing red strings on their wrists or rocking Evil Eye repellent necklaces. No protection at all. They figured what use was it, hell was already on Earth. And that mentality carried over to '96. And fun fact, Tupac died from Mal de Ojo too.

The thing about Mal de Ojo, you don't know you got it until you got it. Well I guess that's how all things are, right? But for us, on this block, bad shit happens all the time. Going against bad luck is our everyday norm, so it usually takes us a little longer to suspect we're cursed.

And Dulce Linda didn't know it. She just saw people hungry. And like the true patrona she was, she put her foot and hasta su sicote in that sancocho. Seven-meats, beef consomé, chicken broth, malanga and every other potato (sweet or not) that she could find, and more.

You ever see someone starving? I'm not talking about that feeling you get when you haven't eaten in a couple of hours. I'm talking about starving, skin tucked into your ribs starving. That was the bloque.

Then the fisticuffs happened. I'm talking Latinos versus Latinx. Jabao versus Trigueño. Cuernu versus Cuernu.

Then the shootings happened.

Rat-tat-tat! Brrrrrrt! Pew-pew-pew!

'Cause being hungry had people on edge and no amount of Snickers could satisfy their hunger.

Then...then! People started eating people! Dulce Linda put an eighth meat into that sancocho. You get what I mean? Aztecan Pozole. Google it.

...

Bahahahaaha! I'm sorry. Pelao Jr over there giving me the most confused face I've ever seen. Cálmate, Bobby.

So as I was saying...Bahahaha!

You got me! Bahahahaa! That never happened. I don't even live on this block. I don't even live in Jersey. I was chillin' on East 188th and Concourse, when a news van scooped me up and offered to put me on TV. Shout out to my Mocanos. San Victeros. BX all day, baby. The Boogie Down Bronx.

To my landlord trying to raise the rent, I read the rent control policy, so stop playing. You can't raise my rent more than 4%, papa.

Yo, Pelao Jr, y'all sell loosies? Baahahaa. Just messing with you. I know that's illegal. Bahahahaah!

THE SHOW MUST GO ON

STROBERI

Wow. Carla Rossi really did that. She got Niña in here to bring up poverty, starvation, and shootings. From the get, I said this TV special was too random and too good. But I figured it was just my natural sense of pessimism passed down from generations of—what did Negrita say again—neglect and disenfranchisement.

"Yooooo, we on TV." Rico rushes to show me a news clip on his phone. "Posted a minute ago."

"Press play, dummy." My annoyance with the Niña setup seeps into my voice.

WHAT. AM. I. WATCHING!?

> *"The imprint of it sloping down their thigh makes them feel sexy."*

> *"Then the fisticuffs happened. I'm talking Latinos versus Latinx. Jabao versus Trigueño. Cuernu versus Cuernu. Then the shootings happened. Rat-tat-tat! Brrrt! Pew-pew!"*

This can't be real. Those snippets make us sound mad silly. "Yo, Rico! This wild."

"Right!?" Rico laughs. "Funny as shit. Oh snap! Is that G-Hombre on TV too!?"

On screen is the footage captured by the Go-Pro they attached to G-Hombre's back, earlier. G-Hombre is doing his job, chasing rats and roaches back into the dark corners of the bodega.

I smack Rico's chest so he could stop laughing. "Yo, don't you see they played us?" I stare Rico down. I know I'm not mad at him but…

As if she knew we were talking about the newsreel, Carla Rossi walks in. "Gentlemen, thanks for the great show. We will continue," she pretends to scratch records like a DJ, "choppin' up those videos." She fake-laughs. "I think we got all we needed for today. It was our extreme pleasure. And best of luck."

"Waiiiiiiiit, wait-wait-wait." I don't even know what I want to say but I can feel myself boiling hot. A pot of rice whistling steam and I'm the con-cón. "You're leaving just like that?"

"Yeah, school is letting out soon. Traffic will be atrocious. Might as well get ahead of it." She signals for the news team to collect all the cameras and equipment in the store.

Traffic? This b—

Before I can get a word in, Carla turns toward the door.

I want to reach out and stop her, but…I can't. It would be unprofessional and rude. And I won't let her get me out-of-pocket. It'd just end up as another outrageous clip for the newsreel. But, oh how I feel my soul stretching out of me to slap this bitch!

I grab a party-size Utz bag of chips and pop it in one squeeze. Game on.

Fucking. Game. ON!

"Rico, open up one of them selfie-tripods hanging on the wall behind you. And get the next vecino in here. We recording our truth."

The Last...
and The First

STROBERI

The vecinos were on a roll. They still didn't buy anything, but they was spittin' lava. Putting flava' into my ears. So much that I forgot about the deal I had with the Jew to sell the store. But he didn't forget.

The suitcase, genuine leather. The cap on his head—which I learned was called a Kippah, after Rico called it a Jewish durag—was some exotic material: crocodile or python. The curls under the Kippah were flourishing. I wanted to ask what hair product he used, because it definitely wasn't Crece Pelo, but he didn't want to hear none of it. Just a "sign here." The contract was in a leather folder too. Like, yo, he was on point! I glanced outside, homie was riding in a G-Wagon. The grajo wasn't so pleasant though. And Rico juggling a Speed Stick and an Avon roll-on behind him was enough stimulant to keep me from passing out. But I kinda wish I did, 'cause I don't know. I learned something today…

"My friend, do we have a deal?" he says. His business demeanor briefly breaking for a fake smile.

Rico, initially unaware that the deal is to sell the bodega, starts to catch on. He sets the deodorant sticks down and crosses his arms, tilting his head. His expression of confusion injects guilt into me.

Do we have a deal? $250,000 for a store that I paid $0 for. Rico would understand that quick come-up. The streets are for hustlers.

I grab a Bic pen, but the Jew wrestles it out of my hand before I can properly grip it.

"No, my friend. You sign in style." He hands me a shiny gold pen that is heavier than an entire pack of Bic pens. Feels like I'm holding the Titanic in my fingers. God damn! I rotate my wrists a bit but I'm really stalling.

Last time I signed a deal too good to be true, I got played the fuck out. I mean, Carla Rossi did pay me. But she embarrassed me and my peoples. And our pride was definitely not in the fine print. Yet, although I'm sure this man will pay me too, he might be sneaking something under my nose. What could it be?

My dad came from the DR to accomplish a dream with this bodega. But that has nothing to do with me. In fact, this bodega robbed me of many hours with my father. Shitty father, great person; everyone else speaks so fondly of him.

When abuelas find out I'm Pelao's son, they reach out for a hug.

The one time I was about to get jumped for my Jordans,

one of the ladronsitos recognized me as Pelao's son and let me go.

This other time, I was chilling at the food court in Newport Mall, texting on my phone when this beautiful girl sat down at my table with two trays of Arby's. I thought I was pimp-daddy smoove, and she was trying to holler. But she opened up the convo' with "your dad did me a huge favor." In the same manner that Yoskar came into the store this morning with the stroller.

My dad kept talking about the community. And to not let the community down. Something that meant very little to me this morning. But after seeing how the vecinos—including those that moved out of the vecindario already—showed out today, I learned my father didn't leave me a bodega; he left me a community.

If I sell the bodega, I'd be selling the last pillar of a community that has low-key always looked out for me. I'd be selling away all the amazing and hilarious stories I compiled after Carla Rossi dipsetted. I'd be…selling all the stories that have yet to be told; all deserving to be heard.

This place…I've hated it for so long. I've judged the people that came in here for so long, too. That now I'm here, one signature away from a quarter-million dollars. One signature away from abandoning my community.

I put the pen on paper (or its heavy ass put itself there). I look into the Jew's eyes. I wonder if he's part of the same crew that bought up the trap houses on Ocean Avenue. Those people take care of their community. Buy out entire blocks for their community. Would he be mad at me if I did the same? If I sign, what would my community be left with? Dispersion?

Continue serving the community. Damn, I dead just heard my Pop's voice! If he watching from above, I'm sure he eagle-diving, bald head first, one-hand out in a fist, middle-finger slightly ajar to land the illest cocotazo on my dome. Like a People's Elbow from the top rope. I flinch.

"I don't think I can sign."

Rico's eyes explode open, and his smile curls up like Cantinfla's mustache.

"My friend, if this is your way of asking for more money, you are mistaken. $250,000 is the best offer you'll get before every realtor and business group waits till the business fails. By that time this place will be worth half of our deal. It's now or never."

Man, he is not wrong. Every month, it's a struggle to break-even. Numbers-wise, this place may not last another year. And the vecindario gets smaller and smaller by the season. Yet, they all showed out today. Even those dispersed to neighboring towns. Because to them, Jersey City will always be their hood. To them, this bodega will always be their bodega. And the corner this bodega resides on will forever live in the joyful feeling of nostalgia. I know this because the spots I grew up on are mostly gone. Newport Mall might as well be Cherry Hill Mall with all its luxury brands. All the Rican food spots are Tex-Mex restaurants with prices meant to keep us out. Developers claim they are making the city better, but they won't admit for who. The mayor claims to be improving conditions for the citizens but the citizens he refers to are the people with money that he has lured in from NYC to buy up all the brownstones and houses in sight. And the bike lanes, let's not even talk about it. But I still remember what used to be. And I'm proud of where I'm from!

"You are right. It's a dying business. But I just realized that it wasn't the money that kept my Pops in here all those hours; it was the people and the impact this place had on them. Things change. Times change. But people still want to belong. This store belongs. Even if it's between shiny new condominiums and expensive rentable scooters. My Pops just never knew how to evolve it. Age evaded his capacity to see, that the vecindario never truly left. They just needed a reason to come back. And that, I will give them."

After the Jew left, me and Rico closed the gates, cracked open one of the bottles from my father's secret stash, and went to work. With the added liquor strength, we moved all the shelving to the side until we had a big empty space in the middle.

"Yo, we can line up rows of chairs here," Rico says.

"Yeah, yeah. And have them facing the counter. Yooooo, we can have the register area be the stage!"

"Wooooord, bro. We can put a stool there with a mic.

And perhaps cut off some of the squares from the…whatever the see-through plastic-square shelving is called on the counter. That way the storytellers got more space to be seen."

"Facts on facts. We can also live-stream the stories and—"

"Gain sponsors!"

"Yo, yo, yo, yo, pass me the bottle. This shit got the answers."

"ROMO COÑÑÑO!" Rico begins to chug the bottle a little too fast, before passing me the—

"Yoooo chill! At least save me a—Mamaguebo!? You drank it all!"

G-Hombre jumps onto the counter. Spreads himself on it. And meows, almost saying, "Goodnight, everyone. Y'all don't gotta go home…but y'all gotta get the—" Y'all know the rest.

THE END,
YET THE BEGINNING

Rico's Poem:
I'm To'Rico
(Epilogue)

RICO

Que lo que, everyone? My name is Rico and this is the first time I've ever done something like this besides the one time I hopped on the intercom at Rainbows in Journal Square to confess my love to this shortie—excuse me—this young lady that I thought was ridiculously fly. So here it goes. Stroberi, dim the lights.

I clear my throat.

I call this piece, "I'm To'Rico."

I'm To'Rico

I may have changed my words up.
My approach,
different.

And I may have become more aware.
My mind,
open.

But GOD DANG! When I see a mamasita with a big
ol' jello of an ass, with butt dimples,
I can't help but think,
"Ay, que rico."

And then I wanna give her some of…
Rico.

Make me wanna take the bus downtown to Torico,
and buy her a scoop of pound cake ice cream.
'Cause that cake … oooof how I want to…
Ahhhhhhh!
Pound it till it's,
mí-o.

Thanks, mi gente. I'll be here next week with a piece called, "It dripped slowly at To'Rico." Think Usher's "My Confession Part II" but remixed by me.

Oh, somebody got next? Aight but let me shine a little, my G. What's the rush?

Her car at the meters? What she doing, a drive-by verse or something?

Who is this she or they? Ayyy, y'all peeped my pronoun usage? Haha. I'm nice wit' it.

Oh Las Mamis got next!

STROBERI, RUNNNNNN!

Tentatively set for

February 2024

(But if you can't wait to read more,
keep turning the pages for two bonus stories.)

People Watching in Downtown

Ariel pretends to fix a flat as he watches them walk past. He overhears gossip about a new teacher at the nearby Montessori and watches cyclists and joggers, dripped down with the latest Nike catalogue, glimmer in the dusking sun.

He doesn't have to pretend because everyone just walks past, but he feels the need to explain why he's there. And less of a need to explain the real reason he is there.

He wants to bellow a stretched-out "yerrrrrrr" or a "qué es la que hay, cabrón". One that could sail across the Hudson to New York in a single breeze, but he knows he'd just sound like a crackhead to the people walking past. Instead, he takes the time to appreciate the New York skyline, considering that on this angle the Empire is still visible.

Off with the old, in with the new, he thinks to himself. For a moment, he can feel the Empire State Building's dilemma: long-time resident forced out of sight by the newcomers that are shinier, grander, and likely backed by bigger pockets.

"Need help, brother?" a passerby says, slapping Ariel back to reality.

Ariel cringes at the word, brother. The inflection, bro-*ther*, and especially the person saying it. Ariel being a second-generation Boricua, two shades from trigueño. And the person, a white man molded from a Nazi cookie cutout. Tall, blonde and way too in shape.

He wishes he could reply, "I'm not your brother," like he would've ten years ago, back when the luxury apartment buildings were empty lots, projects, and condemned brownstones. Yet, he bites his tongue because he wants to remain hidden. "Thanks, but I'm all about done." He points at the tire that was never flat.

He stands up, giving the impression that he's leaving, but he's just waiting for that bro-*ther* to disappear at the waterfront's bend.

Why does Ariel stay longer?

Even he doesn't know.

His childhood home—which he thinks he's parked in front of—is a wild guess. The street numbers aren't the same. The sidewalk that he snuck his name into before the cement dried when he was ten, has been repaved with a bike lane. And the skyline has changed so much that he can't position himself directly across Chelsea Piers like he used to as a child.

But one thing he knows for sure though...one of his scheming vecinos must have secured city-sanctioned low-income housing in one of these bitches.

Poor Ariel. He doesn't know... his old home is actually two blocks away.

~

"Dammmmmn, babe! That was a good one. Okay, okay. My turn. You see that couple across the grass near that big boulder everyone is taking pictures on?"

"The yuppies with the dog in the stroller? Shit, that dog got a better haircut than me!"

"Haha, yep. This is what they are saying…"

~

"O-M-G, Honey. That guy over there fixing his flat is so ghetto!"

How to Bag a Shortie at a Basement Party in Another Town

Rule #1: Don't go solo. Well, make your entrance solo, but let your boys go in first. It's your turn to get some action anyway, so just follow the script.

They will scope out the party while you dog the Brugal Añejo with the netting still on so the ladies know you Dominican-Dominican—not that fake I live in Amboy, Dominican. They will text you where the flyest shortie is situated. They will definitely text you which shorties appear to come with trouble: ex-boyfriends, cock-blocking older brothers, etc. Because last time when it was Popola's turn (your best friend who got thin lips that look like a—you know—popola) y'all ended up with bruised ribs from the Timbs stomping. And if they slick enough, they may even bless you with a clandestine picture of whatever cuerito they got lined up for you.

No lie, you guys are really professionals at this point. The HR team of easy bitches with a recruitment rate of fifty percent. So you trust each other's judgement. The biggest protest will come if they send you a pic of a chunky one. But after many hours of scientific deliberation, the squad has determined that the chunky ones are the most likely to get a **BBL** in the future. So the assumption is, if you hit chunky, you'll hit when that cuerpazo has logged five-hundred phantom gym hours. And when you show her off to your uncles at a barbecue ten years from now, they won't know the difference.

Once the squad has found the shortie, they'll position themselves at each corner of the basement. Some real military, Call of Booty tactics. And when you walk in.

When.

You.

Walk in...

...she'll take notice, immediately. 'Cause they will **YEER-RRRR, AYOOOO, OH SHIT HE'S HERE** so loud that everyone is going to search for who got the bellacos excited. But act cool like you actually a big deal. Like someone used to that sort of attention, 'cause they're not done yet.

Your boy closest to la freca will say your name so damn loud that everyone will think it was the voice of God, choosing you as the next messiah.

So now that she peeped you (or at least knows you exist), you gonna lift that Bruggie bottle with the netting like an Olympic torch so she knows you got a bottle on deckie. If it's a blackgirl, tell her it tastes like Henny. If it's a whitegirl, tell her it will fuck her up more than Everclear. And if it's a Latina, just pass her the bottle. She probably has more chest hair than you.

Next, you and your boys will chill near shortie. You're gonna bump her by "accident" and offer her a Bruggie shot out of courtesy. If she says, No, tell her you taking two shots. One for you and one for her.

If she takes the shot, mingle. Vibe her out.

If she grabs the bottle and starts chugging, abort mission. Esa tipa will ruin your night faster than an unexpected case of diarrhea. Plus, you guys made a pact: never bag a borracha. Because there is a clear difference between shortie regretting sex with you because your dick-game wack, and shortie being violated while blacked-out because you're scum. So again, avoid at all costs. Everyone at the party looking for peepee, toto, or culo anyway, no need to be gross.

She may be feeling nice already, and if she Bori or campesina, she gonna play-hit you (with her heavy hands, of course) after your every joke. And after the second hit, once you solidify that she indeed is play-hitting you, you pretend it hurts. So do your best to exaggerate like you auditioning for the WWE. Once she embarrassingly apologizes, you will laugh so she knows you just teasing. *That's* when she gonna realize that you're flirting with her and begin inputting the raw data into whatever toto-granting equation she got for someone like you. She gonna input that you're not a local, but somehow people were dumb excited to see you. She gonna input that you came in with a bottle, so you break the rules. She gonna input that you a funny guy.

New guy, popular, bad boy, and funny. The cheat code to some panties.

If only it were that easy.

This is when the real work starts. Because while you have a clear goal for the night, she likely has one too. If she thinks you cute, but thinks your friend is cuter, alley-oop her to your friend. What does it matter, anyway? They always go for him. And this is the tenth time it being your turn, yet you have yet to bag a shortie.

INSPIRATION FOR
The Last Bodega in Jersey

My father owned a bodega on 85 Franklin Street, Jersey City, which, as a chamaquito, I spent quite some time at. I remember the people that would come in and out. They'd tell stories, complain about el súper, gossip, and drink beers on the low. I remember the water-ballon fights that would occasionally go down at the school (PS No. 8) on the adjacent corner. I even remember seeing Alfonso Soriano, the Yankee second basemen, once, as he visited a family member's nearby home. Listen, if you know, you know; la bodega attracts customers, locals, and chisme, like a ghetto lighthouse. So I figured, what better setting for fictional stories than a bodega? Any story I'd write, no matter how far-fetched, would be believable if I said I saw or heard it at the bodega. Because Disney isn't the only place where anything is possible; everything is possible at the bodega too. ANYTHING...

Fun fact, as of the time of this writing, my dad's old bodega is now a coffee shop called Froth on Franklin. And most of the surrounding area has gentrified in recent years. But in a positive plot twist, the coffee shop is owned by a family of long time Jersey City Heights residents. I love to hear it. Locals striving in a gentrifying environment. Kudos to them.

ABEL VELOZ is the author of *Son of a Mujeriego* (2022) and that one primo that you *still* don't quite know how you're related to. A First-Gen Dominican-American hailing from Hudson County, NJ. When he writes, he wants you to feel like you're at a summer barbeque, family reunion, or chismeando with fulano at the bodega. Same Spanglish, same people, nothing white-washed.

He previously worked in Military Intelligence (Army Veteran), holds a MS in Global Affairs from Rutgers University, and speaks Mandarin.